PASSAGE OF REVENGE

Toby Sanders

Cover design by the author

ISBN: 9798863378589

Published by Amazon

FROM THE AUTHOR

Thanks for looking at my book! I'm a passionate self-published author on a mission to share my unique tales with readers like you. If you've enjoyed the journey so far, I'd be honoured if you could take a moment to leave a review on Amazon. To connect with my Amazon page, simply follow me on Twitter (X) for a quick and easy link @Toby_Author.

For Sedge, Theo & Elba

CHAPTER 1

"Are we good? Awesome. How's the lighting? No, leave the AC running. It's hot as balls today..."

The tall reporter with his movie star good looks took a moment to run a hand through his long, straight hair, pushing it back away from his forehead towards his crown. His eyes caught for a moment on the chrome cufflinks that secured each sleeve of his well-pressed shirt and in a moment of inspiration, he fiddled the silver bars out and began to roll each sleeve up, leaving the folds well below his elbows.

"Casey? How does that look?"

Casey nodded "Good. Casual, but interested. Relaxed, but professional."

"Good. What's the time?"

Casey rolled his eyes, slipping the thick black watch off his left wrist and passing it over "You tell me, Tagg. You're the genius here."

Tagg fastened the strap around his wrist, seeing that ten minutes still remained before his guest was due to arrive. He cast another, nervous look at the two plush armchairs that sat bathed in the glow of the studio lights, not quite facing one another but not quite apart. Just close enough for an intimate conversation that the complex bank of cameras and microphones would record in infinite detail.

"Tagg?"

Casey was peering behind one of the lowered blinds, watching the dusty lot out the front.

Tagg looked at Casey in sudden panic, one hand frozen in his long hair "Shit! Is it him? He's early! I'm not ready..."

Casey dropped the blind and looked sceptically at him "Of course you are! What else are you gonna do?"

"Are the lights okay? I don't know about the chairs..."

"Dude." when Casey was sarcastic, he stood with his hands on his hips, his shoulder length black hair framing his eyes. Whatever cutting jibe he was about to deliver was cut short by a firm rap on the door to the makeshift studio. Three sharp knocks, evenly spaced and as Tagg's eyes widened in nervous fear. He could imagine the visitor stepping smartly back and perhaps folding his hands behind his back as he waited patiently.

"Okay... Okay-okay-okay!" he wrung his hands for a minute.

"Dude!" Casey's voice was sharp.

"Oh! Right..." Tagg hurried over to the door and hauled it open, the winning white toothed smile that he'd been working on since sophomore year pasted onto his face only to find himself blinking stupidly in the white-hot sunlight.

A figure, silhouetted against the glare stood expectantly and as Tagg blinked, he saw it shift minutely, perhaps in sympathy to his discomfort.

"Er - Detective Harmann?"

"Were you expecting someone else?"

The tone was pleasant, cultured and educated with the barest hint of polite humour. A tough sounding voice of a man well used to hardship yet at the same time conveying a confidence that whatever words were spoken, they would be well received.

"I - er - no! I..." Tagg tailed off then abruptly shoved out his hand "Tagg. It's a real pleasure, Detective Harmann."

The Detective's grip was firm and strong, wasting no time on the elaborate shakes so favoured by the state politicians who held court only a block from this small rental unit. Instead, it was a firm single pump with a grip that did not crush Tagg's own strong hand but certainly let him know that it had the potential to do so if it chose to.

"Won't you come in out of the heat?"

"Sure."

"A coffee? A glass of water? We've got some soda on ice."

"A glass of water'd be fine."

Tagg hurried to the makeshift bar and scooped up a well-polished tumbler, filling it with water from the refrigerator. His hand shook as he poured and he took in a deep breath, willing himself to be calm.

"You know -" Detective Harmann was saying from somewhere behind him "- I thought I'd come to the wrong place at first. Right part of town - if you know what I mean - but maybe the wrong block." Harmann's deep drawl was not unfriendly.

Tagg turned around, pasting the well-practiced smile back onto his face as he held out the glass "Sure, it's not City Hall but we all start somewhere, don't we?"

"Absolutely." Harmann conceded, taking the glass and in that smooth exchange, Tagg felt his cool settle back over him and the smile came naturally. He watched Harmann sip the water and held out a polite hand, inviting him to take a seat.

"AC alright for you?" he asked.

"Just right."

"That's a snappy jacket you're wearing." Tagg eyed the well-tailored sides of the Detective's sports coat.

"That's mighty kind of you to say." Harmann plucked at the neutral grey fabric "Had it custom tailored just a half hour or so from here. Webb & Co., maybe you'll drop them a mention when this goes out?"

"Sure thing. Webb & Co. you say? Sounds British to me."

"Oh, I think it was once upon a time. Maybe way back when but now it's good American made gear." Harmann unfastened the single button deftly as he took a seat and peeled back the lapel to reveal a series of complex looking pockets from which protruded the accoutrements of law enforcement.

"Is that one of those tactical pens?" Tagg pointed.

Harmann popped the device out "Sure. Made by Gerber."

"Would you remind me what those are for?"

Harmann gave a smile "Well, they're mighty handy for writing a word or two." he chuckled at his own joke and Tagg smiled "This tip here? That'll get most panes of glass smashed in alright. Can't be doing without it in my line of work." he tucked the pen out of sight.

"I wonder if you'd talk me through some more of your gear? You know, just so we can get a good measure of one another."

"Are the cameras rolling?"

"Casey?"

"No, they're not until I tell 'em to, Detective."

"Good."

Harmann stood up from the armchair and pulled both sides of his jacket back and began pointing to objects "Service weapon - that's a Glock 19 by the way - this is a torch - Streamlight Protac." he flashed a dazzling beam on and off making Tagg blink "A good blade – this here's a Wilson Combat folder made by Fox Knives outta Italy." Harmann flicked a small black blade out with a deft movement of his wrist and held it out for Tagg to admire.

"You're certainly well prepared, Detective."

"Can't be any other way in this job."

"Can I ask how many times you've had cause to use that service weapon?"

"Oh, a few times, I can tell you." Harmann gave a weighted smile and nodded "This thing's saved my life more'n once. But you know that, being a local?"

"Oh, I'm from the east coast." Tagg smiled apologetically, knowing how much heritage meant to people in this state "Moved here for college and never left."

"You carry a weapon though, don't you?" Harmann's face was concerned.

"No, Sir. Never seen the need."

"Well young man, it ain't about the need as much as it's about good common sense. State like this, we're a freedom loving people and that means we respect our constitutional rights, but it also means we got our fair share of bad guys. And they like guns too."

Tagg nodded.

"There's a mighty fine place on 51st and main that'll set you up nicely with a sturdy second hand one of these." Harmann tapped the Glock, leaning forward in the chair to do so "You tell 'em Detective Harmann sent you and you'll do just fine."

"Well, I'll be sure to head down that way this afternoon, Detective. Thanks for the tip."

"You can park right out the back of the home supplies store next door, if you need."

"I'll do that."

"Well, alright then. Now, don't you got some questions to ask me?"

"Sure. Casey?"

"All ready! Action on your mark."

"Ready." Tagg straightened his back, glancing once at the camera and propping the single page of notes he'd prepared on his knee.

Casey held up a hand, five fingers extended and began to count down silently, finishing in a closed fist and pointing at Tagg who smiled at his guest, putting the cameras out of his mind.

"Detective Harmann. You've been the lead investigator for the State Appropriation and Theft Agency for how long?"

"Well, I took up with the SATAs about thirty years ago now. Been lead Detective for oh, twelve years." Harmann smiled.

"And it's not been a quiet career, has it Detective? Plenty of people in your position would've taken a nice desk job by now, left the hard work to the fresh-faced youth." Tagg smiled as he spoke, ensuring the question was phrased as a compliment.

"Sure, more'n a few have too. But I like to think my job is out there in the heat, catching bad guys."

"And how many have you caught to date?"

"In total? Oh, four hundred thirty eight. By my count."

Tagg's eyes widened in mock surprise although he'd researched Harmann's record meticulously before he asked for the interview "Well, that's an incredible number. I think the only thing I can say is thank you for your service, Detective and I'm sure anyone watching this would say the same."

Harmann smiled modestly and said nothing.

Tagg flicked a glance at his notes and held the next question in his mind, working the phrasing out carefully "What is it, Detective, that you'd say is the reason the SATAs have had such a high rate of success, compared to say, local law enforcement or even the FBI?"

Harmann nodded magnanimously "That's a good question. Now you've gotta understand that in this state, we're one people. Sure, we might have different backgrounds - my family are German - but we're all from here and that means we know how we think. But there's an old saying 'Once a thief, always a thief' and from my experience, it's only the stupid people who break the law."

Tagg nodded encouragingly, not taking his eyes off Harmann's own.

"And so, if you're stupid enough to steal, you're stupid enough to get caught. And around here, we don't like criminals. So maybe you manage to pull something off - bank robbery or some such thing. Maybe a few days or weeks later you're in a bar shooting the breeze and you let the booze get the better of you and run your mouth. I'll tell you, it happens all the damn time - like I say, these people are stupid!" Harmann leaned on the word, steel in his voice "Round here, someone'll hear you and they give me a call and they say 'Hey, Detective. Got you another one of them dumb a-holes down here' and next thing you know, we got another dumby doing time." Harmann sat back with a self-satisfied smile.

Tagg felt the answer in his mind, resisting the urge to frown "So, it's relying on the great people of this state that's the secret to SATA's success?"

Harmann blinked several times and then frowned "No, that's not what I said. My point is that any criminal is dumber than a cop."

Tagg nodded, moving on "Could you tell us about a few of your biggest hauls, Detective?"

"Oh, there have been a mighty few big ones." the smile was back in place "There was the TT gang - buncha British guys outta the Isle of Mann over there. Rode bikes - fast ones. They'd come over here, knock over a few banks and get out on the bikes. Damn they went some speed on the blacktop!"

"How'd you catch them?"

Harmann nodded, smile firmly bolted on now "Glad you asked! We used some good old fashioned American ingenuity. They had bikes, but we had choppers and guns. Can't outride a helicopter and we went and followed 'em until they ran outta gas. Got their little vacation extended by fifteen to life!"

"And am I right in thinking that was the first case you were lead investigator on, Detective?"

"That's right but that was a walk in the park next to my second case."

"Of course!" Tagg glanced at his notes "The famous air jacking of flight 72A9."

"Oh yes! It's another great example of how criminals never outsmart the law."

"I understand though that this was a copycat crime of another famous case - an unsolved one - the D.B. Cooper case?"

"Yes, but I solved this one."

"That's for sure, Detective! Maybe you could explain the D.B. Cooper case for folks that don't know?"

A benevolent smile crossed Harmann's face "Sure. D.B. Cooper was the alias of a gentleman who climbed aboard a passenger flight back in the 70's and midway through, handed the stewardess a note saying he had a bomb and he was gonna blow them outta the sky unless they paid his ransom. 'Course, he was as dumb as the rest of them. Asked for a parachute and then jumped out right into a hell of a storm, over the middle of nowhere and no-one ever heard from him again."

"He was never caught?"

"Nope. Feds got all involved, but they never found zip."

"But with your case…"

"Glad you asked! This suspect went aboard flight 72A9 in Denver and about thirty minutes into the flight, he hands the stewardess a note saying he's packed a bomb in his luggage and told her they were to land the plane here in the state international and they had to bring a ransom aboard along with a couple of parachutes."

"And the plane did land, didn't it?"

"Sure. It landed alright at the 'national and a certain Detective carried the ransom money aboard." Harmann grinned modestly.

"Wow." Tagg made sure his gaze was enraptured.

"Anyway, it was simple. I got my service weapon in his face and that was that. He's doing life for grand larceny."

"That'll certainly put any more copycats off!" Tagg smiled to himself as the Detective nodded with a self-satisfied expression "Now, I want to ask you about a case that I and the public hold dear to our hearts. This - ah - real nasty piece of work called Dunn. William C. Dunn?"

Harmann's smile faded and he shifted slightly so that his face was turned more towards the cameras. He folded both hands in his lap and cocked his head slightly.

Tagg pressed on "William C. Dunn is on the FBI's most wanted list as well as being wanted in most states, including here by the SATA. Could you tell us why that is, Detective?"

"Because he blasted my partner, Detective Jerry Kaminski in the face in cold blood." there was no mistaking the cold fury in Harmann's voice "Let me tell you, young man and let me make this a public service announcement to anyone watching. Dunn isn't his real name but it's one he's known by in a lotta places. This man is the incarnation of pure evil. He'll do whatever it takes for him to come out on top. He's still at large solely because of his brutality and his willingness to kill and maim those in his way. By our count, at least ten innocent people lie dead at his hand and more than a dozen more have suffered life changing injuries. Four of those killed were law enforcement officers who he gunned down without a thought for the lives he ruined and the families he tore apart."

The room was silent, filled with a chill that had nothing to do with the air conditioner quietly humming above the window.

"Jerry Kaminski was at Dunn's mercy. He'd lost his gun,

nothing he could do but let Dunn go and the bastard kicked ten kinds of hell outta him before shooting him in the head at point blank range. He could've just left him, it didn't make a difference to him getting away but he did it because he enjoys it."

"Now, his description is circulated everywhere and there is one simple way to deal with him. If you see him, you put a bullet in him and ask questions later."

Tagg swallowed, the steel in Harmann's gaze unsettling him. He nodded at the words, more for the benefit of the camera's than anything else. A question rose in his mind and he paused, wondering whether he dared push the dangerous looking man sitting opposite.

"But don't you want to bring Dunn in? Don't you want to see him go through the judicial process? Hasn't he done enough to earn a death sentence?"

Harmann was already shaking his head "Son, there are times in our lives when we have to take action, to make a stand and if William C. Dunn is in your sights, that's one of those times. That man is a menace and is no use in this life."

"But isn't that contrary to what law enforcement is all about? Protecting and serving?"

Harmann slapped an angry hand onto his own thigh "Son, I can tell you're not from around here! That's the kind of attitude they take out on the east coast, where things are safe. Out here, we're still living on the frontier and men like Dunn are everywhere! Now, the state sees fit to execute people sure enough but only after years of our tax dollars funding a cosy little prison cell and making sure he's fed and watered better than your average 'Nam vet living on the streets. No, Sir! This is a case where the barrel of a gun is the only option."

Tagg wasn't sure what else to ask. He felt the interview was at an end but he didn't know how to tail the conversation off. Fortunately, the Detective leaned forward to help "Look, how about I show you what I'm talking about? We've a... job we're doing this week. How about you come for the ride along?"

Tagg gawped at the man "I - er..."

"I ain't that unusual to have the press with us! Look, if you wanna get the point of what I'm saying you've gotta come see it for yourself. Think how good that'll look on tape!"

Tagg wanted to consider but Casey was nodding vigorously from behind the camera and apparently, Harmann thought that was it.

"It's settled then!"

"Won't it be dangerous?" blurted out Tagg.

"Sure! But you'll be with me and remember, no thief is smarter than a cop!" Harmann sat back in the chair, that self-satisfied grin well in place on his face.

"Well, ladies and gentlemen there we have it, Detective Harmann of the SATA's, a great American hero. Stay tuned for footage of Detective Harmann in action, coming right up."

"Aaand cut!" snapped Casey and Tagg sat back in the chair, sighing with relief.

"What are you gonna title it?"

"Huh?" Tagg was confused by Harmann's question.

"The interview. Why don't you call it 'No thief is smarter than a cop' - Detective Harmann of the SATAs." he moved a hand across the air in front of him as he spoke, illustrating the headline.

"Er - sure." Tagg blinked several times at the terrible line.

"Good! Now, I've got work to do. I'll have one of my guys give you a call tomorrow and we'll set up this job. You'll come too?" this was addressed to Casey who nodded vigorously.

"Fine. Have yourselves a great day now."

Harmann left, leaving Tagg staring after him, not quite sure what he'd just gotten himself into.

CHAPTER 2

"What a fucking jerk!"

The voice was slurred by alcohol and muted by the jarring music that filled the humid bar. The speaker, a tall white man, shot a look at the stark Navajo features of the barman.

"You see this, Ray?"

"Yup."

"Guy's a real piece of work, huh?"

"Sure, is." Ray vanished behind a cloud of cigar smoke, the billowing gray rising to partially obscure the 'No Smoking' sign above his head.

"'No thief smarter than a cop' - what's this buttmunch talkin' about?" when his loud voice failed to raise a response from Ray, the tall man directed his voice across the bar "Ey - Charlie! You hear this shmuck?"

"Whole bar hears it, Tom." said Charlie, quietly.

"Whaddya think? Think he's talking outta his ass?"

"Sure, Tom. Outta his ass."

"Yeah!"

The other patrons cast their eyes down, not wanting Tom's wide lips to steal their attention away from the glasses they nursed.

"Someone oughta teach that guy a lesson! Mebbe set him up and take him down a peg or two!"

Ray puffed smoke and turned to refill the glass of one of the silver haired men who took up semi-permanent residence at the bar.

"Y'alright, Darell?"

"Sure am, Ray."

"Good."

"Ey - Darell! What d'ya think about this Detective asshole?"

"'Think it's too damn hot for all that jawin', Tom. Why don'tcha keep it down a little?"

A general muttering of assent from the older patrons which set Tom to angrily muttering into his beer as he swigged. On the ceiling above, a weak electric fan pushed the humid air and cigar smoke around. The TV bolted to the wooden panelled walls droned on through the news channels, highlighting the upcoming raid the Detective was leading. Tom swigged his beer in the heat and the yellow nectar loosened his tongue. Ray stood silent behind the bar, eyes locked on the TV and the older men had stepped out to fire their guns into the dirt, a much-loved past time. Tom fingered the varnished handle of his own revolver for a moment but the sullen expressions of Darell and his cronies dissuaded him. Instead, he directed his voice towards the only other occupant of the bar south of fifty.

"Charlie - how's the kids doin'?"

"Gone to Bucksville to collect Grandma."

"They doin' alright in school?"

"Not too bad, Tom."

"You gonna bring 'em down to the range soon?" Tom ran a popular shooting range at the edge of town which was a favourite haunt of the locals.

"Sure."

"How longs your Ma here for?"

"'Bout a week. Got her house up for sale. Wants to move closer to us."

"Good. Best place on earth, this town." Tom slapped the carved wood of the bar appreciatively. On the screen the rolling ticker tape gave details of the raid the Detective would be partaking in and Tom peered blearily at it.

"Say, Charlie. Why don'tcha bring your Ma and the family down the range Wednesday? We can get around the big screen down there and watch this thing."

Charlie considered. The Range held the biggest TV in town,

well known by the kids who were usually dropped in front of the oversized cartoons it was normally tuned to whilst their parents shot their guns at Tom's range. On the other hand, it would mean an evening in Tom's overbearing company but a second later, Tom turned to Ray.

"You'll come too, Ray? Bring Darell and a few of the boys."

"Sure."

"Well, alrighty then! Got us a regular old par-tay!" Tom grinned and knocked on the bar for another beer.

CHAPTER 3

Tagg licked his lips nervously and pushed his sunglasses further up the bridge of his nose where the sweat had loosened the frames. He glanced around at the heavily armed men and women surrounding him and reassured himself that he was as safe as could be. His hand fiddled with the velcro fastening of the ballistic vest Harmann had given him with the word 'PRESS' stencilled across it in bold yellow letters. As the big Sergeant at the front turned to check his team, Tagg suddenly wished the letters were not so bold, nor so yellow. Surely, he'd be the first target?

"Hey man." he heard the quiet greeting behind him and turned to see Casey shaking hands with Harmann as he balanced his complex camera equipment on his shoulder.

"Alright, boys. How ya doin? Hot as hell out here, ain't it?" Harmann was grinning with an enthusiastic energy which Casey returned. Tagg felt a stab of jealousy that his cameraman / producer / director / buddy was getting along so well with the subject of their movie. After all, he, Tagg was supposed to be the charismatic reporter and Casey should just be hanging around out of sight. Instead, Casey and Harmann seemed to have bonded and Casey now sported a new lump beneath his shirt from the matt new Glock he'd purchased just the day before. Tagg had gone with him to the store but had baulked at the prices and left empty handed. He hoped Casey would keep his hands on the camera and off his piece. There were enough guns around them.

"All ready, Detective." the big Sergeant from the local PD had approached, a long black shotgun held in both hands. Harmann gave a nod and then gestured for Casey to roll camera.

"So, what we're here for today is to catch a gang of armed robbers in the act." he addressed Tagg with frequent glances at the camera where Casey was giving him a grin and thumbs up "Now, we know how these guys work and we know their M.O. This right here is their first escape route" Harmann gestured for Casey to film up and down the dirt filled alleyway they crouched in "Second, is gonna be over that footbridge and down the creek to a vehicle they've already parked there. Now, we've got a team down there and we've disabled the vehicle."

"Wouldn't it be safer to have a team by the bridge? Catch them early?" Tagg tried to ask an intelligent question, feeling well out of his depth.

"Sure, but it's safer not to try and pin them down. When we get them, we want them to know they're surrounded." Harmann's face became sombre for a moment and he looked straight at the camera "We do things by the book here. The aim is to stop the bad guys and make sure no-one gets hurt in the process."

"Good." Casey gave another thumbs up and Harmann grinned, happy with the take.

"Suspects sighted." another officer, finger pressed against a radio earpiece tapped Harmann on the shoulder.

"Alright! All teams to standby." he ordered and the officer relayed it. Tagg felt sweat bead on his forehead and beneath the vest.

The sun beat down and the officers sweated. Casey jigged his foot up and down, a stupid grin on his face.

Suddenly, the officer with the radio grabbed Harmann's arm "Detective - suspects are entering from the rear of the building."

A flicker over Harmann's face, quickly recovered for the camera's sake. The big sergeant moved closer "That leaves us without a covering team. I say we call it off!"

Tagg found himself nodding in agreement but Harmann shook his head "No! I'll take these two -" he indicated the two nearest officers "And flank them. That'll cut them off and send them the way we expect. You continue as planned. Send that to the other teams." he nodded to the officer with the radio who began speaking into the headset.

"That's not protocol -" protested the Sergeant but Harmann got in his face, ignoring the extra foot the Sergeant had on him.

"This is my raid, dammit! I'm in charge! Now shut up and do what you're told!"

To Tagg's surprise, the Sergeant melted before Harmann's wrath and the Detective nodded in satisfaction, beckoning his two officers forward.

"Come on!" with a start, Tagg realised Casey was urging him after the Detective and he swallowed, took a breath and then hurried after the Detective, crouching awkwardly as he ran.

"Here!" Harmann pulled him down in the vague shelter of a dusty yellow patch of shrubbery. Ignoring Tagg, he gripped Casey and pointed through the foliage. Tagg peered after the camera and his breath caught as he saw the back of a square, red brick building. The back wall was clear aside from two rusting dumpsters which rested against the brick, either side of a green painted fire door which was propped open with a crumbling breeze block.

As Tagg stared, an engine sounded and Harmann pulled him down, pointing eagerly as a car pulled into view, a late model sedan in black. Nondescript.

What was not nondescript was the two men who climbed out, paused to look around and then began striding purposefully towards the open fire exit.

"Now?" whispered one of the officers and Harmann gave a half nod but then held up his hand, glancing once at the camera which Casey was training eagerly on the two men.

"Wait..."

"Jesus! Is this dude crazy?" thought Tagg as he realised that Harmann was trying to maximise the sensationalism of the robbery for the sake of the camera but there was nothing he could do except sit back and watch as the two men cautiously approached the door, pulled it fully open and vanished inside.

"Okay, let's move!" Harmann was up, pistol drawn and already moving as Tagg stumbled after him. They reached the door and Harmann flattened himself against the red bricks, already looking back for Casey. Tagg reached the wall only to have one of the other officers, this one sporting an M4 style rifle, shove him out of the way.

"Me first! You two come after." Harmann indicated Casey and Tagg didn't protest.

"Now!" Harmann was in, quickly followed by the rifleman and then Tagg followed, eyes blinking stupidly in the sudden dim lighting of the interior.

He was aware of the pleasant cooling sensation on his skin from the air conditioning, the sight of Harmann ahead of him, pistol extended in a two-handed grip and then he heard voices shouting and suddenly the officer with the rifle was speaking into a radio loudly, caution abandoned.

"All teams move! Move, move, move!"

A gunshot sounded from ahead.

Then there was screaming.

CHAPTER 4

The big Sergeant with the shotgun was called Reyes and he was still staring mutinously after the hot-headed Detective when the radio crackled and the unmistakeable boom of a shotgun came from within the building.

"Shit!" Reyes, surprisingly nimble for his size lead the way towards the building at a dead sprint, shotgun tucked against his chest. He sweated under his body armour as he moved, slowing his pace as he reached the door to the bank. His shoulder slammed against the wall as the next officer tapped him and then Reyes was through the sliding door, erupting onto a scene of utter chaos.

Four men, two wearing black ski masks and two plain faced were clutching weapons. One - Reyes had to blink to believe it - was wielding some type of AK, a second held a pump shotgun and the other two had handguns. At the sound of the door opening, all faces turned to the big Sergeant and stared stupidly down the barrel of the shotgun.

"Everyone FREEZE!" Reyes bellowed.

A fusillade of pistol shots sounded, not from the four robbers but from behind the counter where the teller stood with her hands over her head.

Reyes swore loudly, twisting aside as the robber with the AK turned, whipped the rifle up and emptied his magazine at the shots.

The others fired at Reyes who fired once, pumped the action, fired again and saw the man with the shotgun go spinning away in a riot of red mess before a pistol fired close at hand.

There was a bang, a terrible flash of light and then an awful burning sensation in his chest and someone was shouting his name over and over.

Reyes did not respond.

CHAPTER 5

Tagg stared in horror as Harmann emptied his pistol. Behind him, Casey was grinning like a madman making sure his camera missed none of it. Harmann finished the mag, swore for effect and stepped back behind the thick wall. He switched his mag and nodded to the rifleman who leaned forward then swore and flung himself back as the unmistakeable chatter of automatic gun fire sounded.

To Tagg, it was like being in a terrible war movie. The bullets tore into the narrow corridor, tearing paint and chunks of brickwork from the wall and forcing dust and grit into his eyes and nose. He crouched against the wall, hands over his head and yelled in terror until it suddenly stopped.

More through instinct than anything else, Tagg opened his eyes to see that miraculously, the bullets hadn't harmed anyone. Through the door he could hear shouts, screams and more gunshots and as he watched Harmann leaned around the door, aimed and fired three careful shots from his Glock.

"He's down!" the Detective ducked back into cover with a wild grin on his face, winking at Tagg as though this were the greatest fun in the world. A whoop of joy sounded nearby and Tagg stared in shock at Casey who was on one knee, covered in dust and chunks of brick but pointing the camera at Harmann as though it were the most important thing on earth.

"This is great, man!" he roared to Tagg as the sounds from within the bank began to change. Screams finished, there were no more shots and orders began to be shouted.

"Clear!"

"Clear!"

"Friendlies coming out!" roared Harmann and a moment later, Tagg found himself staggering forward after the Detective as they emerged into the chaotic scene.

There had been half a dozen patrons in the bank and the single teller. All of them were now on the floor, cowering in terror. Police and SATA agents swarmed like locusts, all of them with weapons drawn. Tagg looked for the robbers and regretted it instantly. One was a tangle of twitching red gore in a pool of blood. A pair of officers were already stood by him but they made no move to help the man who, even as Tagg watched, stopped twitching. Nausea flooded through him and he turned to Casey who was still wearing that shit eating grin.

"This is great, man! I'm telling you!"

"Get a fucking hold of yourself, Casey! That guy just died!"

"Yeah, so did that guy!" Casey gestured with his free hand and Tagg turned to see a man with a Kalashnikov lying next to him bleeding freely from a head wound. His eyes were wide and staring and Tagg gasped in horror.

"I got that guy!" Harmann was pointing at the dead man, something close to pride on his face. He still clutched his service weapon and gestured with the gun, making Tagg wince as the barrel whipped across the room.

"EMT's!" shouted someone and Tagg was shoved to the side as two stretcher teams ran in. First, they stopped by the bulking Sergeant from before who Tagg now saw had the name 'REYES' across his chest. He was breathing fitfully, the front of his body armour buckled from a gunshot. Tagg saw no blood and hoped the man would be alright but the medics quickly took him off to the waiting ambulance.

"Over here!"

Tagg turned toward the voice, grateful for the distraction from the exuberant Harmann who was dancing around like a kid on Christmas. The second team of EMT's were crouching by the counter behind which the teller still crouched, whimpering. Tagg wondered when someone would tell her it was all over.

But it wasn't the teller the medics were looking at, neither was the officer who had called them over. Instead, they stood staring in silent horror at the awful sight of the small, twisted body that lay still beneath the counter. At first, Tagg thought it was a child and then he was relieved when he saw that it was in fact an elderly woman, twisted with age. Instantly, Tagg felt horrified at the relief he'd felt. The woman was dead, blood soaking her elegant grey curls and crusting in the string of pearls around her neck. She wore a pink blouse and smart black slacks over a pair of old, but well-chosen black heels.

There was blood everywhere. On the blouse, on the slacks and trickling down past her heels. Tagg felt his feet move although he wasn't aware of telling them to. As he drifted forward, unable to take his eyes from the woman he saw that her face was well made up. He wondered if at her age, going to the bank was still a thing to dress up for, that she might have been planning to call on a friend in the neighbourhood and had made an effort to look nice.

Her face was heavily lined and her eyes were closed. If it were not for the blood, she could have been sleeping. She'd been wearing a pair of old-fashioned spectacles, secured around her neck by a thin black cord and they had slipped down her nose. Tagg had an absurd urge to push them back up onto her eyes but he was scared it would be disrespectful.

"Goddamn." he muttered and the nearest EMT caught his eye, nodding.

"Hey - hey, Tagg!" Casey tugged his arm, trying to get his attention.

He got it. Tagg rounded on his friend, gripping him by the arm hard enough to make him yelp in protest "Hey! What's your damage, man?"

"This is! This is my goddamn damage, Case! Where's that goddamn motherfucker? Harmann!" he bellowed the name and the Detective came over, uncertainty on his face for the first time.

Making sure Casey had the camera on him, Tagg pointed to the old woman "How do you explain this? Why did you let these men come into a building where innocent people were?"

Harmann gave that self-assured smile "That's protocol -"

"No, it isn't! I heard your Sergeant - Reyes! - telling you that outside. Why did you break protocol? You cost this woman her life!"

"I didn't shoot her!" protested Harmann, lamely.

Tagg stopped, looking from the old woman to the doorway behind the counter where Harmann had stood.

"Casey! So, the Detective stood there -" he pointed "- this old lady was stood here -" he grabbed the lens and pointed it at the corpse "And those two guys -" he pointed to the two men with pistols who had been cuffed and battered by the other officers "- were shooting that way. Towards Reyes!"

The room had gone very quiet. All eyes were locked now on Harmann who was staring at Tagg, murder in his eyes. Tagg was suddenly aware that Harmann still had his weapon in his hand and he blinked several times, licking his lips and looking from the camera to Harmann's Glock.

"It was him, man! He -" the voice was cut off by a thump and a grunt of pain and all eyes turned to the nearest of the two surviving robbers who had shouted. The obese patrolman who was kneeling on his back had just thumped him in the side and the thief's eyes watered with pain.

Harmann took the distraction in his stride. He holstered the Glock, turning to yell orders.

"Get these assholes out of here! Get them locked up and get their rights read! Everyone else, start taking statements! You!" he pointed at the EMT's "Get her out of here, right now! And you!" this at Tagg in a voice so laden with venom that Tagg actually took a step back "Get the fuck outta my crime scene!"

Tagg, closely followed by Casey, got the fuck out.

CHAPTER 6

"Hey, man. You wanna tell me what the fuck just happened in there?" Casey's voice was controlled but Tagg could hear the shock in it.

They were walking away from the bank, roasting on the sidewalk under the hot sun.

"Just shut up, Case. Goddamn. I need a goddamn drink." Tagg realised he was still wearing the body armour with the yellow stencilled lettering and in a sudden fury, he ripped the velcro off, tossing the vest onto the sidewalk where his sweat fizzed in the heat.

"That lady -" Casey began again but Tagg rounded on him.

"Just don't, Case! Alright?"

"Okay! Okay, man. Just take a breath." Casey held his free hand up, palm facing forwards "Look, our truck is right around the block. Let's go there, drop this sucker off -" he hefted the camera "- then we can go get ourselves a nice cold beer and take a look at how this just went. Sound good?"

Tagg nodded "I wanna go back to the studio. We've got beer there."

"Fine. So long as there's beer. Now, pick that up before we get busted for it. Place is swarming with 5-oh." he risked a glance around before tugging his sunglasses from his pocket and pushing them over his eyes. Tagg made to do the same but realised he still wore his own frames. His eyes widened in surprise as he realised he'd left them on throughout the whole raid.

They turned and began walking down the long sidewalk. Despite it being the middle of the day, no-one was around.

The sound of gunshots and Sirens tends to clear the streets as effectively as a curfew. A few parked cars baked in the heat but no-one came towards them. They moved in silence and reached the truck which Casey unlocked, hefting his camera inside. He took the flak jacket from Tagg and tossed it in, both of them climbing into their seats.

"Hey man, you did good today. That was a tough gig. Let's go break ourselves for a bit, huh? Try and forget it."

"Yeah."

Tagg started the engine and muttered something.

"Wassat now?"

"I said, I don't want to forget it. That lady didn't need to die."

"I know man, but that don't bring her back –"

"I ain't trying to bring her back, Case."

"Then what're you doin'?"

Tagg told him.

CHAPTER 7

One week later

The scene in the bar had changed only a little. The slow-moving fan futilely pushed the humid air downwards only to meet the oppressive stink of Ray's noxious cigars. The old TV bolted to the wood panelled wall crackled on, CNN blaring out although no one in the bar was listening. Darell and his group of silver haired cronies had moved around one of the lower tables and were quietly passing cards back and forth. Ray kept silent vigil behind the bar, moving only to light a new cigar or pour another drink. Tom perched on the other side of the counter, his eyes flicking from the TV to the corner where Charlie sat motionless.

"C'mon, Ray, let's change it over, huh? See if there's a game on?"

Ray stabbed a stubby finger at the remote and the channel switched, a local news station rolling into play.

"… more on the bank robbery shootout that left three people dead including one innocent bystander, seventy year old Mavis DeLayney who leaves behind eight grandchildren, her brother and her two grown up children."

The newscaster turned expectantly to her partner.

"That's right, Dianne and here we see from our very own reporter on the ground the startling footage that we've been seeing for the past few days which appears to show how the carelessness of Detective Hartmann of the SATA resulted in this needless death."

"More than a few critics have spoken up, revealing how Detective Harmann has been reported on multiple occasions by fellow officers for breach of protocol, thereby endangering the lives of his fellow officers and the people of this great state who he swore to protect and serve."

"Well, it's hard to see how this could be any worse but Deputy Director Finnick of the SATA has reassured the public that a full and thorough investigation is in progress and that the agency will get to the bottom of this awful tragedy."

The story changed and Tom tapped the bar with his knuckles, shooting Charlie a glance "Good! 'Bout time they took that prick down a peg or two!".

He spoke too loudly but Charlie's only response was to stand up and stalk out, loudly slamming the door behind him.

Tom stared after him in consternation, eventually turning an aggrieved expression to Ray who shook his head.

"Let him be, Tom."

Tom bent over his drink, his brow furrowed as he silently fumed.

The door swung open again, admitting a blast of heat that made Tom fully appreciate the little work the weak fan did for him. Behind the bar Ray vanished in a puff of cigar smoke and Tom turned to the door, expecting to see a conciliatory Charlie. Instead, two men stepped in, one dressed in the shorts, sliders and sleeveless top of a hipster, complete with the beard and earrings and the other in the semi casual dress of an office worker or a politician, high-necked polo shirt tucked into khaki's with impeccably clean tennis shoes.

Tom gawped at the pair as they entered and even Ray waved a lazy hand to dissipate his own cigar smoke. The sight of two new patrons was simply too surprising to be unremarkable.

"Help you?" Ray asked as the hipster, sunglasses still firmly in place approached the bar, looking around at the rustic interior with obvious delight.

"Got beer?"

"Comin' up." Ray vanished beneath the dirty wood, returning a moment later with two cold bottles which he rested on the worn edge of the bar before banging the tops off, sending them spinning to the floor and out of sight.

The hipster gestured for his friend to find a seat and Tom watched in amusement as the smartly dressed young man paused to kick a speck of dirt off his shiny shoes before lowering himself into a booth, facing away from Tom.

The hipster followed a moment later and Tom, still staring, leaned closer into Ray "Hey, Ray. Ain't that the guy off the news? The guy that got this out?"

Ray puffed furiously on his cigar for a moment and then without answering, added a generous shot of bourbon to Tom's empty glass. Darell came by and Ray popped four more beers for the older men and Tom accosted the silver haired man.

"Darell, you reckon that's the guy from the news?" he pointed before knocking back the shot.

Darell took his time turning to the booth where the two younger men sat before he responded, all while Tom drummed his fingers impatiently.

"Sure, could be. Sure as I am that it ain't polite to go hasslin' new folk in old Ray's bar here. Ray's gotta business to run ya know."

"I'm gonna find out - hey! You! Smart-boy!"

The smartly dressed man actually jumped, leaning out of the booth to see who was shouting. His eyes widened in surprise when Tom looked at him and he glanced around, making sure there was no mistake.

"What?"

"Ain't you the guy off the news? Tags or somethin'."

"Leave the man alone, Tom." Darell protested.

"I'm just bein' friendly, Darell!" Tom protested.

"C'mon man, let's just go." muttered Tagg but Casey had stood up and turned around, hipster glasses finally pushed up off his face.

"Yeah, he is. We're the ones that broke the story last week. What's it to you?"

Tom eyed the younger man for a moment, seeing the angry challenge in his eyes. He was drunk enough that he felt his own emotions piqued and he slowly stood up from his bar stool, making sure the younger man saw the revolver he wore on his hip.

"Ain't no thang." he leaned on his southern drawl to accentuate the point "I'm just bein' a little friendly, that's all. Got me a friend of mine'd like to talk to you boys."

"Sit down, Tom." Ray's voice snapped suddenly from behind the bar. Tom turned to give the old Navajo a withering glance, but Ray's eyes were locked on him like bullets and he suddenly remembered that the man had run dive bars his entire life and had buried bigger and badder men than he, Tom. Besides, it was too damn hot for a fight, so he sat down. Casey sat down too and Tagg pushed the beer towards him.

"Ain't no offence meant, friend." Tom called out but Darell shushed him and pondered over to the booth, standing with his back firmly to Tom and speaking in a low voice so the drunken man couldn't hear him.

Tom muttered to himself for a minute more before he reluctantly turned back to the TV, doing his best to put the men out of his mind. Ray pushed another drink in front of him, a cold beer this time and Tom accepted it as a peace offering. Ray had changed the channel and there was a ball game on. Tom nodded in contentment as he sipped the beer and relaxed as he absorbed himself abusing the players on the screen.

It was ten minutes or so later and he'd almost forgotten Tagg and Casey when abruptly he heard a footstep behind him. Turning in surprise he saw Tagg stood a foot away.

"Tom, isn't it? My name's Tagg. I wonder, would you introduce me to your friend? I'd like to hear what he's got to say."

Tom smiled, a little drunkenly before easing himself down off the bar stool "Well, smart-boy, you're in luck. I think you and my ol' pal Charlie might like what each other's sellin'."

CHAPTER 8

"Detective?"

The polite voice of the young officer brought Harmann out of his reverie. He smiled politely at the auburn-haired beauty of Probationary Detective Moore.

"Everything alright, Moore?"

"Yes, Sir. The forensic lady is ready."

"Oh. Wonderful. Thanks for letting me know." Harmann stood up from his sideways perch in the passenger seat of his car and stretched his back in the sun. Moore had turned and was moving away back towards the crime scene but before she'd even cleared the fender of his sedan, he called her back.

"Moore! Why don'tcha come with me? You might learn a thang or two." he spread his most charming smile over his face and the pretty young redhead smiled in pleasure and followed him.

Goddamn me you are a fine piece of ass! Harmann thought to himself, intentionally holding back a step or two and leering at her buttocks from behind his sunglasses. When she turned around to see where he'd got to, he smiled apologetically and hurried to walk beside her, thanking his lucky stars that she'd been assigned to his tutelage. With a bit of care, she'd be assigned to his bedroom if he played his cards right and he grinned at the thought.

His mood turned as they crossed the sidewalk and ducked under the police tape that barred the entrance to the bank. A uniformed officer nodded unnecessarily to him as he passed, causing Harmann a moment of intense irritation.

Who the fuck are you nodding to, asshole? This is my crime scene!

He kept his better thoughts to himself and rewarded himself with a final look at Moore's behind as he removed his sunglasses, stowing them carefully in his lapel pocket, surveying a scene that was becoming all too familiar.

"Detective Harmann, we seem to be seeing a lot of each other lately." the forensic specialist wore blue gloves and a white overall and did not offer to shake hands.

"Doctor Gilruth, what do we got?"

"Same as the last three." she gestured around the interior of the bank, which was a modern building, low ceilinged with bland cream-colored walls and a thick sheet of glass separating the tellers from the customers. Aside from the huddle of uncomfortable looking patrons and the presence of so many law enforcement, it could have been a normal morning at the bank.

"You took a little time getting here?" Dr Gilruth did not sound accusatory and Harmann dipped his head in acknowledgement.

"Sure. I had to go to a hearing. Internal thing."

Gliruth raised an eyebrow so high that it vanished beneath her white hood "Oh?"

Moore chirped in, her voice filled with enthusiastic joy "Detective Harmann was cleared of all wrongdoing."

Bitch, you stole my goddamn thunder! thought Harmann to himself but he did not begrudge Moore her moment of jubilation, enjoying the happiness she showed at his success.

Gilruth fixed him with a hard stare, peering through her clear glasses "Well, congratulations."

Harmann smiled and changed the subject before her sexless demeanour could ruin the moment with Moore "No fingerprints?"

"Still finalising everything and we'll go over the security footage to make certain but no, don't think we'll get anything this time either. Oh – no plates on the bikes they rode, by the way. I already checked."

Harmann ground his teeth at her presumption, but he managed an even tone when he spoke "Alarms were cut again, I see." he looked to the teller, a skinny brown faced youth who looked not a day out of high school.

"Nope." Gilruth shook her head "My guys said the system works fine. Teller didn't trip the switch."

"Huh?" Harmann stared in surprise "Why not?"

"You're the Detective." Gilruth turned away as one of her team drew her attention, their features hidden behind the white coverall and goggles.

"C'mon." Harmann led Moore over to the teller who had produced a Yoohoo from behind the counter and was now swigging deeply as a local cop waited patiently.

"Hey!" Harmann did not touch the local guy, but he made sure his body language excluded the cop and included Moore as he let his eyes bore holes in the unfortunate teller "You wanna tell me what stopped you from hitting the alarm? Sat behind three inches of bullet proof glass and you did what, offered the guy a goddamn Yoohoo?"

"Detective -" the officer began to protest but Harmann ignored the man.

"I - I'm sorry!" the young man had a dribble of chocolate milk on his lower lip and was wide eyed in shock at Harmann's attitude.

"Well, you'd better have a good story for your boss! Can't say I'd want a pussy like you working in my bank!" he snapped "You know that because you didn't hit the button, these guys got away? This gang have been knocking over banks for weeks now and because of morons like you, we've got exactly squat on them! What's wrong with you?" he turned away for dramatic effect and rolled his eyes in affected exasperation at Moore who stood with her arms folded beneath her breasts, all but shaking her head at the teller.

"Moore, you make sure this officer gets a full statement!" he delegated, stepping away to survey the crowd of patrons who were still being questioned. Abruptly changing his demeanour, Harmann approached a blonde-haired soccer-mom who was holding the hand of a bored looking ten year old.

"Good morning, ma'am." Harmann affected his best drawl and

aw-shucks smile, making sure he got as many of his straight, white teeth in as he could.

"Oh! Good morning."

He flashed his badge, making sure she saw the grip of his Glock as he did so "I'm Detective Harmann with the State Appropriation and Theft Agency." recognition flickered in her eyes and he saw the odd nervousness that affects ordinary people when faced with a celebrity. He smiled inwardly "This is a fine young man!" he addressed the ten year old "What's your name, son?"

"Michael."

"That's a good strong name. Man's name. How old are you, Michael?"

"Eleven."

Only a year wrong.

"I'm Mrs Adamson - Cherie! Call me Cherie." Cherie was blushing and stammered slightly.

"Well, Cherie, that's a mighty pretty name." Harmann had learned long ago that direct compliments to married women were usually taken as offensive whereas an indirect piece of flattery was charming.

"Why, thank you."

"By the sound of those tones you're a local lady?"

"Yes - I mean I'm from out of town but lived here for - for some time now." she smiled widely.

A bit too friendly thought Harmann *Dial it back a bit, lady. I ain't tryna bang you.*

"And you came in to make a deposit this morning?"

"Oh, no I came to speak to the manager. This branch are supposed to be very forthcoming with business loans."

"Oh, you're an entrepreneur?" Harmann slapped on a few more teeth to the smile.

Cherie gave a loud and modest laugh, actually flicking her hair a little "Oh! I wouldn't say that. I run a handful of dance classes around town in the schools. I was hoping the bank would give me a few dollars to buy a new sound system."

Harmann was only familiar with one type of dancing and it was not the same as Cherie's classes so he dodged the subject "This branch is nationwide, I believe?"

"That's right. They have a lot more scope for the smaller loans because of that. Of course, I'd have loved to have gone to a locally owned business, but they just don't have the same ability."

"They sure don't." whatever that meant "Cherie, I don't suppose that you got a look at the men who came in here?"

"Oh, I did. One of them talked very nicely to Michael. You'd hardly believe they were robbers the way they spoke."

Resisting the urge to roll his eyes Harmann turned to Michael "What about you, sport? Did'ya see their faces? Notice anything about 'em?"

"They were on motorbikes. So, they wore helmets." the kid looked at him as though he were retarded. Harmann forced his smile a few degrees wider, realising he was getting nowhere. Moore chose that moment to provide a useful distraction, begging his attention and he bade Cherie and her ugly brat his most charming southern farewell before stepping away with Moore.

"Well?"

"Apparently it's bank procedure for the employees to comply with any robbers."

Harmann stared "What's the bullet proof glass for, then?"

She shook her head "I don't know. For show, maybe? I asked to speak to the manager but there isn't one or - there is, but he manages a dozen branches across the state and only comes in once a fortnight. It's pretty much autonomous." she gestured to a row of booths with touchscreen monitors in them "Most stuff is done through those. The teller is really only here to lock up at night and answer the odd question or help the older clients."

An image of the dead old woman flashed through Harmann's mind and he squashed it, surprised that such a thing would bother him now.

"Detective?" Moore was looking at him.

"Say that again, would you?"

"I said the thieves just took the cash from those machines. They didn't touch the vault."

"They didn't touch the vault? How much did they get then?" Harmann was confused, the report had said a big robbery.

"Like I say, most of the transactions are done through the machines so they actually have more cash in there than in the vaults."

"Goddamn! That is about the dumbest thing I've ever heard!" Harmann shook his head at the stupidity of cost cutting corporations as Moore nodded sympathetically.

"Anyway, I got the manager's number. You want me to call him?"

"No. Give it here." Harmann pulled out his cell and dialled the number which rang to voicemail, so he left a message with his name and number before rolling his eyes at Moore.

"I got that guy's statement." she put in, referring to the wretched teller.

"Good." Harmann glanced at the teller who had finished his drink and was now looking around sheepishly "He have anything to say about the bad guys?"

"Not much. Bike helmets, coveralls and gloves, same as the other three. Only one gunman again. Oh - said this time the gun was pointed at the ceiling the whole time."

"What? He didn't even point it at the teller?"

"Yup. Just stood there looking tough whilst the other two emptied the machines."

Harmann put his hands on either side of his head and squeezed his eyes shut in consternation "How in the hell is this even a bank robbery? It sounds more like a damn charity donation!"

Moore nodded sympathetically, her red hair bobbing as she did so "Life would be a lot easier if people would stand up for themselves."

"You got that right. Goddamn." Harmann glanced around the scene, suddenly frustrated with the entire proceeding "Hey, you wanna get a cup of coffee?"

"Sure." Moore suddenly looked sheepish "I er – I haven't had the time to read the reports on the three other cases, I wonder if you wouldn't mind briefing me?"

Harmann actually felt a pleasurable shiver run down his spine at her invitation. He flashed the toothy smile at her again before gesturing for her to lead the way out of the crime scene, turning his back so the officer on guard couldn't nod to him again.

CHAPTER 9

The coffeehouse had air conditioning, three pretty baristas with big smiles and the lovely warm aroma of freshly brewed beans. Harmann paid, sipping his unsweetened americano whilst Moore surprised him by opting for a double espresso.

"Late night?" he asked as he left a big tip, making sure Moore saw.

"No! I like my coffee strong." she knocked the small drink back whilst Harmann sipped his and winced at the heat.

"I can't help thinking, Detective how similar this is to a previous case you worked on."

"Sure. The TT gang. You read about that?"

She looked mildly embarrassed "I wrote my final essay about it in the academy."

He paused, coffee raised halfway to his mouth "Oh? What did you say about it?"

She was blushing now, the color accentuating the light lipstick she wore and the freckles on her cheeks. Harmann found this extremely attractive.

"I pointed out how in many cases the investigators try to follow the pattern and chase down leads - to put themselves in the minds of the suspects."

Harmann waited.

"But you didn't, you cut to the chase - literally - and decided to take a risk."

"By letting them complete the robbery?"

"Exactly. Not many Detectives would allow the crime to take place. They'd grab the guys beforehand but by waiting until the crime had taken place, you allowed them to think they'd got away and then they got sloppy."

Harmann smiled benevolently and launched into an unnecessary retelling of the story, complete with action, helicopter chases and the final climactic moment where he'd roared through a loud hailer at the gang to surrender.

He was interrupted by the peal of his cell phone and picked it up to discover the bank manager on the other end.

"Sir –" Harmann affected his strictest tone "Would you please explain to me the logic behind telling your staff to simply stand there and hand over the money?"

"Sure." the voice on the other end sounded unconcerned. The sound of a vehicle running at speed told Harmann the manager was driving with the cell on hands free "It's bank policy. We're insured up to our eyeballs and honestly? A single branch getting hit isn't even a blip on the radar. The forms have already gone in and we'll have a pay out by the end of the week. No-one got hurt so frankly Detective, we aren't that bothered."

Seeing Moore looking at him, Harmann decided to lay it on thick "Sir, let me tell you that this is a serious crime. These men have committed a number of these offences already and they're armed and dangerous. I don't see -"

The manager cut him off "Yeah, I know all about it, Detective. They hit another one of our branches last week nearby. Didn't you hear about that?"

Harmann frowned "Last week? That wasn't one of yours."

"Bunch of assholes on racing bikes? Sure it was! We trade under a couple different names in the state. Keeps the bosses up top happy and the customers think they're getting that local service still. Same body, different faces." Harmann fancied he heard the grin on the man's face.

"But I didn't speak to you last week?"

"No, Sir. You woulda got the assistant manager. I was taking a personal day."

"And you didn't think to speak to law enforcement when you got back and found out one of your branches had been robbed?"

"What can I tell you, Detective? We're insured, the money

comes back in the end and business is still business! It's all good!"

Harmann hung up, thoroughly annoyed.

"These goddamn companies don't care!" he raved at Moore.

"Seems like it's only us who wants to catch the bad guys."

"What d'ya mean?"

"Everyone in that last bank kept saying how polite the suspects were. That older lady you spoke to seemed like she might vote for them."

"Cherie." he murmured.

Moore looked surprised "I hadn't realised you took her details."

Harmann realised it was a rare slip up and he hastened to cover it up with some of his default bluster. Goddamn, but Moore was just so hot he couldn't keep his thoughts straight around her! He either needed to bang her or take a cold shower. Or maybe both.

"Should we go back and work on this some more?" she asked.

"No." the conversation with the manager had soured his mood and he stood up abruptly "I'm gonna go see some people about this case. You go back to HQ and start working on a report. I'll see you later." ignoring her surprised expression, Harmann left and drove himself home.

CHAPTER 10

"Get it damn well fixed, Harmann!"

"Yes, Sir." Harmann's tone was only so subdued and courteous when he spoke to his boss. No-one else, from state officials to senior law enforcement ever heard him speak this way but then, he reflected, no-one else signed his pay checks.

Finnick leaned back in the plush leather armchair behind his mahogany desk that Harmann knew had been a donation from a wealthy family in town who liked to keep law enforcement on the friendly side.

"Ah, heck. We been workin' together long enough Harm. What's bothering me is how much it seems like these sons of bitches are aiming at you."

Harmann nodded. The thought had occurred to him.

"I can't remember such a successful string of copycat crimes. It's like they saw that damn interview you did and they're reading it like an instruction manual. Next thing you know, you'll be busting my budget on helicopter chases again. I don't know, Harm…"

Harmann, standing before the desk with his arms folded over his groin held his breath, waiting to hear what Finnick would decide. He had a great deal of respect for the old man but in the past few years, the Deputy Director's caution had been getting the better of him. It chafed Harmann who liked to think of himself as a man of action and what had for the best part of twenty years been a relationship based on mutual respect was now well on its way to a natural end. Harmann knew Finnick only had two or three years left before retirement and he had his eyes on the polished black surface of that desk.

"I wonder if we shouldn't take you out of the firing line, Harm."

Harmann ground his teeth and forced his tone to politeness before he responded "Sir, with the greatest of respect, I disagree."

To his surprise, Finnick smiled "Thought you might."

"Look, Sir. You know how I operate. I bust asses and don't waste time. These guys with their racing bikes and smooth talkin' might think they're hot young shit but I'm here to show them they're just another bunch of brain-dead morons who weren't smart enough to hold down a real job."

"I know who you are, Harm. But you gotta see this from my perspective." Finnick sighed and rubbed the front of his desk thoughtfully "Look, in a few years you could be sitting where I am."

You're goddamn right I will. thought Harmann, viciously.

"And from here, you can't look at these cases from the barrel of a gun. Now - don't argue - I ain't sayin' you don't get results. We both know you're the best damn investigator the state has ever seen. That ain't in question. But what we got here is a public image problem. This reporter fella... Taff?"

"Tagg."

"Tagg. Whatever. He got that story out and it don't matter that he weren't right about it. It ain't what the public knows, it's what the public thinks and you know as well as I do that people in this state love to see the little guy get one over on the big guy. If it's states against Uncle Sam, you know we'll always back the state. Same here. These guys are making a mockery of you by pulling this off and I'm worried that it don't matter whether you catch 'em or not. Public still gets its image and then I got the governor and the Director up my ass telling me to get this no-good Detective off their damn TV screens."

Harmann felt a wave of misery wash over him. He cursed the bureaucratic minds of men and women in politics who gave a damn only about what voters wanted. Didn't they see that he was at war here? The sons of bitches with their flashy motorbikes were openly mocking him by copying the exact details of the TT gang he'd busted all those years ago. He cursed the memory of his interview with Tagg.

"And then there's this guy Dunn." to his credit, Finnick shot Harmann a sympathetic look "Now, I know as well as you do the best thing that sonofabitch is a .45 to the head. I knew Jerry Kaminski too and I want payback as much as you! But that ain't how the law works and you upset a lot of folk with that public service announcement you did to Taff or Tagg or whatever his name was."

"I know and -"

Finnick waved him to silence "I know what you're gonna say, Harm so save it. Fact is, people associate you with him now. He's 'your guy'. Even in the agency! Don't look at me like that, Harm, you'd think the same! It's how we work."

"Sir, Dunn hasn't even been confirmed to be in the state! All we have is one patchy eyewitness report and that shit-eater Tagg got hold of it and sent it to the news channels."

"I saw the report, Harm. We all did."

"So? Why can't we go after this guy Tagg? You ask me, that's where all this is comin' from. What's he got against me, anyway?"

"He thinks you shot that old lady."

"Well, I didn't. And that was proven in a court of law."

"It was proven in an internal investigation - oh! I know. Relax, Harm." Finnick held up both hands as Harm's face flickered with anger "That ain't the point. Point is, I gotta do something about this or we all go down the can."

Resigned, Harmann waited for Finnick to tell him the decision he knew the old man had made long before he summoned Harmann to his office.

"Don't look like that, I ain't gonna get rid of my best investigator. Look, the Fed's called in a favour up in Montana. They got trouble of their own up there - crossed state lines or somethin' and they asked for someone and you ain't doin' no good down here."

"Montana?" Harmann had never visited the northern state.

His face flickered in distaste.

"Yeah, yeah. I know. Look, it ain't gonna be for long." Finnick had leaned forward onto his elbows, the smooth grey of his suit reflected in the shining surface of the mahogany "Think of it as a vacation! A chance to clear your head, get away from these damn fools on bikes."

When Harmann looked morose, he rolled his eyes "Look, Harm. You said it yourself. What's that line you came out with?"

"No thief is smarter than a cop".

"Exactly! And these guys knocking these banks over, they're just a bunch of freakin' morons! They aren't worthy of our best investigator. No, I don't want you wasting your time over them. Go catch some real bad guys and make us look good with the Fed's, huh?"

Harmann knew the words were just flattery, but he let them wash over him, consoling himself.

"Alright. Take the rest of the day, Harm. We'll get you on a plane tomorrow."

Harmann nodded and turned to leave the Deputy Director's office, but a thought occurred to him and making his face as innocent as possible, he turned back to Finnick.

"Sir, I don't suppose Probationary Detective Moore could be assigned with me? She's a hot - bright young officer and some time with the Fed's would do her good."

Finnick shot him an evil grin "Oh, I bet it'd do her real good!" he dropped Harmann a hearty wink "You take her and run her through the case then, Harm."

Harmann left the office, a small smile playing on his face. At least his exile would give him ample opportunity to work on getting Moore out of that tight pant suit she wore. He pictured her lying naked in a hotel bedroom next to him, her red hair spread out on the pillows and a leer crossed his face.

"Everything alright, Detective?"

She made him jump and Harmann blinked fast several times, trying to reconcile the image of Moore in the flesh before him, pant suit intact and push the image of her nude body from his mind. Recovering quickly, he pasted his winning smile onto his face.

"Pack a bag, Probationary Detective. We're goin' to Montana!"

To his pleasure, a grin flashed across her own face and as she turned to gather her things, Harmann resisted the urge to pump his fist in the air and whoop. Montana, here he came!

CHAPTER 11

The name on the man's drivers' licence was Russell Howard but that was only one of the many names he'd collected over the years. This one, he'd stolen from a British comedian he'd seen on TV in a cheap bar in Las Vegas just before he'd had to flee that city when the heat got too much.

It was a point of pride to him that there were few states where he was not a wanted man. As he crossed state lines, he avoided cops and officials as a rule, hiding his features behind a series of elaborate disguises. Today, he wore a dirty baseball cap pulled down low over his eyes and a short but fake salt and pepper beard reaching up to his hairline. This, combined with slacks instead of his preferred blue jeans and a windbreaker even in the heat, gave him the look of a man twice his age and he made sure to walk slowly as though his joints were stiff.

In this state, he was wanted under the name William C. Dunn and following that interview from that asshole Detective, he'd found life more than a little uncomfortable. Fortunately, his quiet intellect and capacity for violence along with a few old prison buddies scattered around had found him steady work, always on the wrong side of the law. But since Harmann had gone on camera to tell the world about his misdeeds, work had dried up and Dunn was pissed.

Pissed enough that beneath the windbreaker, clutched through the sliced lining of the pockets he held a Colt 1911 with a full magazine. It wasn't his weapon of choice, he preferred to kill with his hands or a good knife, but he'd fired enough rounds over the years to know how deadly he was with the handgun. More to the point, this one had been cheap, unregistered and well kept. He'd stripped it down and oiled it a few times, taking it out into the desert for an afternoon to run it through its paces, ignoring the cost of each bullet he blasted into the sand.

The SATA building loomed overhead, a towering monstrosity of oppression and evil to Dunn. He'd learned about the Nazi's in prison and had watched a movie all about Adolf Hitler and in his mind at the top of the SATA building sat a small man with a funky moustache, ordering his minions out to kill men like Dunn.

But not today.

Dunn had been loitering here ever since he'd seen Harmann go inside earlier that morning. He'd kept a loose tail on the Detective for a couple of days, figuring out where he lived but after analysing the guy's route to work, he was pretty sure this was the safest place. Despite it being a state building, the armed guards stayed inside, behind the revolving door and out of the heat. They were at least fifty feet away and by a pure stroke of luck, Dunn had seen an older lady trip and fall almost outside the building just the day previously. It took the guards almost a minute to run outside and help her and he had a car parked right in front of him. After firing and hitting Harmann, he reckoned it would take him less than ten seconds to drive away.

A cop approached him as he sat on the warm bench, but Dunn didn't worry. Two of the officer's colleagues had passed by already, including one in a squad car who had lit his roof up and shouted at him. Dunn didn't worry about the gun in his pocket - there was nothing illegal about carrying a concealed weapon and his licence would pass any checks the officer cared to make. So, he sat unconcerned as the officer drew level and then, realising the man was not about to stop him, he nodded a greeting to the cop.

"Good morning, Sir. Fine day, ain't it?"

"Sure is."

He wondered if the cop would stop to chat and what he'd do if Harmann came out the building whilst this guy was still here. He figured shoot Harmann first and deal with this guy second. The cop wouldn't be expecting an older looking guy to pull a weapon and if necessary, Dunn could always run across the street to make sure Harmann was dead. He'd still have time to get away but fortunately for him, the cop moved on and a moment later, he was out of sight.

Dunn released his grip on the pistol, allowing it to rest on his bare skin beneath the windbreaker, which was truthfully, far too hot for this weather. He fished a pack of camels from his pants pocket and kissed one out, lighting it with relish. He blew smoke, leaning his head back to peer up at the azure sky where a bird circled. A vulture? He didn't know many birds, but he chuckled to himself for a moment at the thought that his old man disguise was so good that the carrion bird was expecting him to keel over at any second.

Lowering his gaze, Dunn swore, the camel falling from his mouth to smoulder beneath the bench, forgotten. Opposite, Harmann had appeared and was already half a dozen steps from the building. His sedan was parked a few bays down but now a voluptuous redhead Detective was walking next to him. Dunn wasted no time gawping at her tits, he hauled the 1911 from his pocket and dropped into a two-handed shooters crouch, barrel tracking his moving target. He grinned to himself as Harmann and his partner failed to notice him, took careful aim and squeezed the trigger.

CHAPTER 12

Harmann realised he was a few steps ahead of Moore and so he paused, waiting for her to catch up and hopefully overtake so he could get another look at what he was taking to Montana with him.

The pause saved his life.

The first .45 round whipped through the air an inch from his nose, so close in fact that he felt the passing and instantly flinched backwards. Thirty years of experience then made itself known as he dropped to a crouch, pulling his Glock from its holster, turning and firing a half dozen rounds across the street.

A second shot from the unseen assailant and then Harmann caught a glimpse of a bearded face, a dark gun barrel and then Moore fired her own piece and the gunman dropped back behind the fender of dark painted car.

"Detective!" shouted Moore and Harmann saw her standing to fire. Seizing the moment, he sprinted to her, sheltered behind an unmarked SATA car parked at the kerb. Part of him wondered where in the hell the armed guards from the Agency were.

"You get a look at him?"

"Baseball cap. Beard. Sounded like a .45."

"Agreed." Harmann risked a peek over the edge of the car only to hear a door slam and see the vehicle which had sheltered his assailant suddenly burn rubber and fly off up the street, away from where he crouched.

"Son of a bitch!" he raised the Glock and fired two careful rounds which struck the rear bodywork uselessly and then the driver flung a hard right on Macey and was gone.

"I got the plate!" shouted Moore and Harmann nodded in

relief as the security guards finally spilled out of the building, shouting and waving their guns.

"He's gone!" he snapped, furious at their tardiness. Still holding his Glock in a two-handed grip, he carefully crossed the street, moving through the empty space where the assailant had fired from. A handful of .45 brass littered the ground and he stepped carefully around them, not wanting to contaminate the evidence.

"Son of a bitch!" he said again, his hands already shaking as the adrenaline left him. A whiff of something pungent caught his nostrils and he turned to the bench, dropping to one knee to peer underneath.

A grin formed on his face.

"Hey, Moore!" he shouted and the Probationary Detective came running across the street, holstering her weapon as she saw him replace the Glock.

"Got an evidence bag?"

"Sure. But shouldn't we let forensics pick up the brass?"

"It ain't for the brass." Harmann leaned under the bench, heedless of his Webb & Co. jacket scraping on the dusty sidewalk. Grinning triumphantly, he withdrew his arm, dropping something into the open bag in Moore's hands. She held it up so she could see the burned out yellow filter of the cigarette.

"Those things'll kill ya!" he joked, grinning from ear to ear.

CHAPTER 13

"Richard F. Berkowitz." Dr Gilruth nodded at the piece of paper she'd just dropped onto Finnick's luxurious desk.

"Who in Satan's asshole is Richard F. Berkowitz?" demanded Finnick who had doffed his jacket and was sweating even in the air-conditioned office.

"It's one of the aliases that Dunn used. Could be his real name." Harmann had controlled his shaking hands and managed to affect a cool demeanour even if his heart was still racing. Beside him, Moore's hair was in disarray and her hands twitched every few seconds. Harmann had thought this would make her less appealing, but he found himself having to work harder and harder to stop leering at her.

"And this piece of trash thinks he can take a shot at a state investigator, outside of our own building? No, Sir! Not on my watch!" Finnick actually thumped the desk. His face was turning an interesting shade of puce.

"Are we certain it's him?" Harmann asked Gilruth who had processed the DNA found on the cigarette in her own lab in just a couple of hours. Harmann was amazed at the efficiency of the doctor and was wishing Finnick would stop panicking and thank the woman properly.

"It's him. We happened to have his DNA on file for a separate case - a mugging - and so we got a match."

"Bastard!" swore Finnick "It must be because of the interview. There's no other way." he turned to Harmann "Harm, you're back on this case. I'll talk to the Director myself and tell him what's happening."

"Where is the Director, by the way?" Gilruth asked. When

everyone looked at her in surprise she shrugged "I assumed he'd be here, an incident like this."

"He's out of state..." Finnick muttered "Anyway, the point is, I'm giving you whatever you want. Men, people, vehicles - get this son of a bitch and teach him a damn lesson."

"Yes, Sir!"

CHAPTER 14

"Detective?" Moore followed Harmann as he stormed down the hallway towards his office.

"What?"

"We don't have any leads."

"No."

"So... What are we gonna do?"

"We're gonna go see that reporter."

"Tagg? What for?"

"Maybe to kick his ass. All I know is, this started since he decided I was the devil incarnate. Maybe he knows something, maybe he don't." he slowed, turning to Moore "Here's a pro tip, Moore. Journalists? Really damn good at finding stuff out. So, when you get the chance, you let them find it. Like this for example." he continued walking "Maybe Tagg and his little hipster buddy don't know nothin' but we go there and put enough pressure on him, maybe he puts a little time into finding out what is goin' on. And then there's this guy, Dunn. He's an evil sum-bitch and I don't think even Tagg wants to see him at liberty."

"We want Tagg to find us a lead?"

"Sure. Now, get your poker face on, Moore. We need to look the part. Got it?"

"Got it."

*

Tagg was in the studio, shirt off in the heat as he tapped on the keyboard of his laptop. His social media following had blown way out of proportion since he'd released the tape of the interview and Harmann's raid and it was becoming a full-time occupation just to manage the various platforms and accounts. A glass of water stood warming beside him and he glanced briefly at the post-it to remind him to call the air conditioning guy.

A noise sounded from outside, a squeak of some sort.

"Casey?" he called. Casey wasn't due back for at least a couple of hours and he frowned, scooting his wheeled chair back and walking over to the door.

Crash

The door swung open, admitting a wave of heat and two suited detectives, one of whom, Tagg had time to notice, was a smoking hot redhead. The other's face was like iron and in a moment of panic, he recognised Harmann who marched towards him, arms outstretched as he herded Tagg back across the makeshift studio.

"You can't just bust in here, man! Back off!" Tagg protested but the woman got in his face and he backpedalled.

"You sit down right here, Tagg and start talkin'!" her red locks bounced as she spoke and Tagg looked at her in surprise.

"Talk about what?"

She made a move as though to step forward and Tagg flinched, fully expecting her to slap him but instead she straightened and towered over him as he tried not to cower in the seat.

"You wanna tell us about these robberies? You wanna tell us why ever since you did that interview, we've got copycat crimes all over the state? You wanna tell us what you got to do with that?"

"What? Aw is that what you're bustin' in here for?" Tagg affected a wounded innocence "You guys don't seriously think I'm involved in bank robberies, do you? I'm a reporter!"

"I think you know something for sure." Moore had put her hands on her hips and still towered over him while Harmann had turned away and was pacing around, just a couple feet away.

"I don't know anything! I mean - I saw the news, sure, but why would that have anything to do with me?"

"It isn't a coincidence then?" she layered sarcasm into her voice "You didn't think you'd get your revenge on Detective Harmann by dragging his name through the mud? You thought that falsely accusing him of shooting someone wasn't bad enough, so you went after his good name instead?"

Tagg's laptop binged on the table in front of him and he glanced at it, automatically. At the same time, his phone buzzed in his pocket and his smart watch flashed with one of his news apps. A local station.

"Hey! Asshole!" Moore snapped as he frowned, eyes scanning the text before looking to the laptop where the full article had popped up.

"Christ! You were shot at? Who by?" he turned to Harmann just in time to see the Detective take three quick strides, shove Moore out the way and swing his leg in a straight kick into Tagg's face.

A flash of blinding white light. The shock of the hard floor on the side of his head and then Moore's voice yelling "What the fuck, Harmann!"

"How'd you like it now! Huh! How'd ya like it now! You son of a bitch!" Harmann was yelling while Moore held him back. Tagg blinked stupidly. He felt like he'd been hit with a sledgehammer. The entire front of his face was throbbing in agony and his nose and lips had gone numb. He breathed in and choked, spitting some sort of liquid out of his mouth. He raised a hand to his mouth and stared in horror at the bright blood covering his palm.

"Outside, Detective! Go and take a breath! Damn!" Moore's voice was filled with fury and something approaching panic. Tagg was vaguely aware of her hustling Harmann away who was swearing loudly.

The door slammed. Tagg coughed blood up and spit.

"Here..." warm hands were on him, helping him up "Here - come on. Is there a bathroom in here?"

He pointed mutely, his lips still numb but his mouth now beginning to throb. Moore half carried him, half dragged him over to the tiny washroom and pulled the light. She ran the faucet, cupping a handful of water and splashing it into his mouth. He gagged and hawked blood all over the white porcelain.

"Hey - take it easy for minute there." a calming hand rested on his shoulder and Tagg forced himself to calm down, breathing slowly.

He spat and tried to speak "That guy is a fucking monster."

"He's... He's a good Detective. Good cop."

"Oh yeah?" Tagg's voice was thick, liquid in his nose and mouth "Thought cops were s'posed to protect you."

He risked a glance in the small mirror, staring in horror at his shattered nose and burst lips. Mercifully, his teeth seemed to have avoided Harmann's heavy shoe, but his tongue had been crushed at the tip and hurt like hell.

"I'm real sorry about this." Moore was shaking her head "I don't know what he was thinking. This isn't me..." she faded off into an embarrassed silence and Tagg realised that she was genuinely upset, trying to apologise. Right now, he was finding that hard to accept.

"What kind of name is Tagg, anyway?"

"Irish."

"My mother was Irish." she pointed to her red locks.

"Was?"

"Is."

"Good for her." he spat a thick gob of blood into the sink. The numbness was starting to fade but, in its place, a burning pain was settling and he winced, squeezing his eyes, embarrassed at the tears that were forming.

"I should get you to the ER." said Moore, straightening up and looking around "Do you have a car out front?"

"It's fine." he spat another gob into the sink "My buddy Casey will be here soon." his words came out thickly and he had to repeat himself twice before Moore got it.

"No, you can't be left like this."

"I'm fine." to prove it, he stood up straight and took a few tentative steps towards his laptop before settling back down into his chair.

Moore followed him, hovering like a nervous parent.

"Did you really get shot at?"

"Yes."

"By Dunn."

"You knew that?"

He shook his head then immediately regretted it and winced at the pain "'Course not. Makes sense though. Guy fucking hates Harmann." he looked up at her from eyes that were filled with tears from his shattered nose "This wasn't me. I'm not a criminal."

She nodded, holding his gaze "I believe you."

"You should go."

"Can I call someone...?"

"Just go."

She sighed, then turned and began to walk towards the door, pausing before she reached it "This isn't me. I'm not like this. This isn't why I joined the agency."

Tagg watched her with sad eyes "It's why he joined though. People like him shouldn't hold power."

Moore turned and walked out into the sunlight, shutting the door behind her. Harmann was leaning against the car, grinning like a schoolboy "Hey! Good job in there. That's the real good cop – bad cop stuff we've gotta do."

"You just assaulted that man."

"Hey, c'mon now! Don't be like that! Remember what's at stake here, Moore! That guy might be a sweet talker but trust me, he's a journalist and he'll do anything for a story! Don't forget that! C'mon, let's go back and go over it all some more."

"Actually, I'm just gonna head home. Get up and start again tomorrow bright eyed." Moore pasted a fake smile onto her face.

"Oh... Okay. I'll give you a ride?"

"Sure."

The car pulled away as Moore pulled her sunglasses over her eyes, hiding herself behind the mirrored lenses.

*

Inside the studio, Tagg picked up his phone and dialled a number manually. It rang once then picked up, the person on the other end saying nothing.

"Charlie? It's me. He just left my place. Kicked me in the freaking mouth. Let's do this, man. Let's do it the whole goddamn way."

CHAPTER 15

The next day, there were no more motorbike gangs holding up banks. Instead, Finnick called Harmann personally to brief him on the latest case as the report came in.

"Are you fucking kidding me?" Harmann actually took the phone away from his ear and stared at the screen as though expecting the caller ID to read 'Prankster'. Instead, Finnick's name stood there clear as day.

"What did you say, Detective?" Finnick's voice held a dangerous tone and Harmann remembered who he was speaking to.

"I'm sorry, Sir. Just a little startled is all."

"Ain't gonna get any less startling, Harm." the Deputy Director sounded sulky.

"Where's the jet now?"

"'Bout thirty thousand feet over us. Air Force got involved, told the pilot he's gotta stay in a holding pattern but he ain't doin' what they say."

"The hell they expect? Guy's got his own skin to worry about."

"Damn straight. Anyway, same detail as the last one - can't believe I'm saying that, Harm. Get yourself down to the 'national. Airport security'll meet you at the terminal."

"On our way. Moore is with me."

"Might be you wanna send her in to the aircraft this time, Harm. Your face has been all over the news lately, if you recall."

"Yes, Sir."

"Credit'll still go to you, Harm. Don't worry 'bout that."

"No, Sir."

Harmann hung up and told Moore to drive to the 'national'

"And put your damn foot down, Probationer."

Moore burned rubber and set the Siren on the roof to blare, the previous day's disagreement forgotten. As she cleared an intersection, blaring her horn at a big rig who shot her the finger she pulled out into the opposite lane.

"You gonna tell me what the fire is?"

Harmann pressed his fingertips into his temples and rubbed them around slowly, apparently oblivious to the fact that Moore was doing ninety on the opposite carriageway.

He muttered something.

"What's that now?"

"I said, son of a bitch has got balls. Flight has been hijacked."

Moore nearly crashed. A minivan blared its horn at her as she braked hard and swerved to avoid it "What in the holy hell are you talkin' about? You can't hijack a damn plane in this day and age!"

"It's not a jet." Harmann grabbed the passenger side handle as Moore spun the wheel "At least - it's not a commercial flight. Small time private charter flights out of - you guessed it - Denver. There's ten passengers on board, none of them appear to know each other. One of them has passed the stewardess a note saying he has enough explosive aboard to blow the whole thing outta the sky."

"And he wants what, ransom?"

"Didn't say. He said the pilot was to land over here at 'national and we'd receive further instructions from there."

Moore swore colorfully. Harmann reflected briefly that the more he saw of her, the more he liked her.

"Is that it?"

Harmann looked out of the window.

"Detective! Is that it?"

Harmann gave a deep sigh as though he were getting very tired of the world "The pilot was asked about the bomber's state of mind and he said the man was 'just really very nice'."

"Oh damn."

"Pretty much."

Moore put the accelerator to the floor.

CHAPTER 16

The interior of the jet was luxurious. Not decadent like the lavish furnishings of an oil sheik nor cheap like the budget carriers who ferried millions through busy airways across the world. Instead, the seats were finished with brown leather which some passengers prodded and touched obsessively, unsure if it was plastic or the real deal. The seats were arranged in rows, although with thoughtful spacing between both the next seat and the one in front.

The man with the bomb sat calmly in the rearmost row, a smart leather suitcase on his lap which was fastened to his wrist with a series of cable ties looped together. A small bottle of water, glass still bearing the condensation from the refrigerator sat open in the cup holder by his seat. He was of tall, with black skin and his age was anyone's guess. Thirty? Forty? He was smiling genially, not forcing his fellow passengers to make eye contact and occasionally sipping from the water bottle.

Maria, the older of the two stewardesses was fifty, already a grandmother and had three decades of turbulence, difficult passengers and fleeting glimpses of faraway lands from her hotel window before she was offered the job with Atlantis 'The small luxury airline'. It had billed itself as a bridge between commercial domestic flights and the unaffordable private charter flights and in the four short years she'd been flying with them, she'd never seen a full flight.

Still, at the prices people were willing to pay, they didn't need to fill every seat and the price point kept away the rowdy bachelor parties and over stressed businesspeople, leaving behind a clientele that were grateful for the extra legroom, the soundproofed cabin and the genuine smiles of stewardesses who weren't overworked.

Now though, as she desperately tried to calm Denise, the younger attendant who'd got the job because she was screwing one of the interns in the employment department - at least according to company rumour - she wondered if another ten years of red eye flights wouldn't have been a better choice.

A small electronic noise pinged on the cabin control panel, drawing her attention briefly from Denise's tears. She glanced at it briefly, looking away before her gaze shot back, locking in horror on the panel.

"It's him!"

Denise paused mid-sob "What?"

The man with the bomb had caught Maria's eye, the gentle smile still in place. He even raised his hand and gave her a small wave, as though to confirm that it was indeed he who had pressed the call button.

"Maria!" hissed Denise, tissue still clutched a foot away from her face, but Maria had stood, stepping past the other passengers who huddled white faced by the stewardesses and purposefully striding the length of the cabin.

She stopped in front of the man and was momentarily flummoxed. How does one address a man with a bomb? But her years of habitual politeness took hold and she found herself pasting a smile onto her lips.

"Sir?"

Had she really just called him 'Sir'? Her surprise must have shown because the black man dialled the smile up a notch.

"Hello. I'm really so very sorry to put you to all this trouble, ma'am."

He really didn't strike her as someone who wanted to kill himself. In contrast, he exuded a kind of savage happiness, as though he wanted nothing more than to be there, on the maybe-leather seats with a bomb cable-tied to his wrist.

"I wondered if could check that my message was passed on to the pilot? You see, I happened to notice we have some guests from our brave service people..." he gestured to the window.

Maria had to crouch to see out the window in this airplane and as she did, she gasped in horror, hand flying to her mouth. Years of being around pilots and aircrew had taught her a thing or two about aviation and she recognised the angular tail fins of an F-35 fighter.

"Oh my God!" she breathed. She twisted her head and looked through the port windows to see a second Air Force fighter, flying just off their wingtip.

"You see, I wanted to check that those brave pilots know it is not my intention to detonate this device." the killer smiled again "I really am not here to cause harm to anyone. It's purely a matter of personal motivation."

"I - I'll check with the pilot." stammered Maria, hurrying across the cabin. In commercial liners, the cabin door is sealed to prevent hijackings but in the small jet there wasn't room for such contraptions but still there were protocols to prevent the crew from bursting in so, as though there were no threat of fiery death a few feet behind her, Maria knocked politely, waiting for permission.

In the cockpit, the captain and the first officer were sweating badly. They both looked up at her with drawn resignation on their faces.

"He - he wants to know that his message was sent properly because -" a sob caught in Maria's throat "Because of the Air Force."

The Captain, a twenty year man named John, nodded then stood up "I'll come and talk to him. You good?" this to the first officer who nodded. The autopilot was engaged anyway and they were at least thirty minutes from their destination.

John approached the smiling man with Maria close behind. He paused slightly further away than the boundaries of normal conversation would dictate as though the extra half a foot would make all the distance when the damn thing went off.

"You had some questions, Sir?"

"Yes, I'm very grateful to you, Captain for taking the time to speak to me. Once again, I'm terribly sorry for the inconvenience and I'd like to reassure you that it's my intention for all of us to walk away from this unpleasantness."

"I understand that, Sir."

"What I'd like to confirm, if it's not too much trouble is whether you're following the request I passed via the wonderful cabin manager -" he caught Maria's eye and gave a charming grin "- or whether those brave men and women of the Air Force have convinced you to follow their procedures?"

"No, Sir. I'm planning on landing at 'national in -" he glanced at his heavy wristwatch "- twenty nine minutes, give or take."

"That's very good to hear, Captain. And have you managed to confirm with the authorities on the ground?"

"Yes. They've agreed to send a negotiator aboard with the cash you requested."

"Bonds, Captain. Bearer bonds. It's essential that they do not deliver cash." his smile turned into a grave expression, not unlike that which Maria used to let her grandchildren know she was serious "I cannot, unfortunately, let a single passenger leave this aircraft if they deliver cash. It must be bonds."

The Captain was nodding hastily, his face looking hassled "Yes. That's what I meant. They said bonds."

"And have you been able to contact your company?"

"Yes. We have a direct line to the company office from the cockpit. They've confirmed that the parent company will be responsible for paying the ransom."

The man with the bomb flicked his smile back on, a flash of white teeth in his dark face. He sat back, contentment on his face "I'm very grateful to you, Sir and to you, ma'am for carrying out those instructions. I cannot imagine how stressful this must be for y'all."

Maria noted the southern drawl which the man had otherwise managed to suppress. His accent had been all over the place, starting with a thick Bronx lilt and even something approaching a bad Australian impression, but she thought that slip at the end was the genuine article and she wondered if the man was a local.

Either way, he still smiled disarmingly as he spoke again.

"I'd just like to triple check if I may, Sir, that it's the carrier - the parent company - rather than this small airline that are footing the bill, so to speak?"

The Captain nodded "Yes. I spoke to the insurance guy from the carrier and he confirmed the process that you detailed in your note." Maria thought she heard a frown in the Captain's voice.

The man with the bomb nodded, gently "One last question if I may be so bold, Captain and then I'll let you get back to the fine job you're doin' of flyin' this here airplane. What did you tell them about me?"

The Captain swallowed, nervously and the man leaned forward, polite concern on his face.

"Oh, Sir, there's no need to look nervous. It's your responsibility to tell them everything you can about me. I just wondered what name and information you gave them?"

The Captain's face twisted as though the next words tasted sour.

"I said your name was D. B. Cooper."

"Thank you, Captain."

CHAPTER 17

Airside at the 'national was a sea of flashing lights and bristling weapons. All flights had been redirected and five minutes ago, two black hawk helicopters had touched down to discharge a host of national guardsmen who now swarmed the place, clashing with the airport police who desperately tried to remain in control.

Harmann had flashed his badge and Moore had driven them all the way onto the tarmac. Operational control of the sea of law enforcement was not something Harmann wanted to be bogged down with and so he made himself scarce when the uniformed commander came looking for him. Instead, he and Moore assumed control of the nervous looking man in the cheap suit who was hurried through security with a sports bag over his shoulder. His ID named him as the insurance guy for the carrier airline - the parent company that owned the smaller operator the jet was flown by. Harmann had kept a hand on the shoulder of the young man, not actually touching the bag he carried but also not relinquishing control.

"We're all set, Detective." Moore took his attention as she stepped away from the communications guy who had finished strapping wires to her torso. She'd left her blazer off to reveal a well-fitting white shirt with her badge and gun well on display.

"Okay." Harmann forced himself to look her in the eye, well aware of how the setting sun was turning that white shirt translucent "Last time - can't believe I'm goddamn saying this - last time, I went into the cabin and pulled my gun. That was it. This asshole knows all about me though. That much is clear from the shot he took at me so me going in there is gonna blow this whole thing up - maybe literally."

Moore failed to laugh at his joke.

"This guy Dunn is a killer. He's capable of blowing the damn jet outta the sky and we ain't takin' any risks. You go in, you give him the cash and the 'chute and you come out."

Moore nodded.

"I don't want to see you in there more than a minute, understand? They ain't gonna refuel so the jet only has about an hour more flyin' time in it."

"What about the hostages?"

"Let 'em out. If he changes his mind, don't argue. You ain't in there to negotiate." Harmann did not admit to himself that he wanted no-one other than himself to dictate terms to Dunn inside the plane.

"Then we're just gonna let him fly off into the sunset?"

"Nope. Air Force is gonna follow him and watch. This guy thinks he's D. B. Cooper? Cooper jumped in a storm, no-one saw him go and no-one saw him land." Harmann gestured to the setting sun which had turned the sky pink, revealing a sky empty of clouds sight "Air's as clear as anything. We'll see him from ten miles away and when he lands? We'll get the motherfucker."

The insurance man looked nervous and Harmann slapped him on the back "Don't worry, pal! We'll have you back with the cash in no time. Give you a good shoe-in for a promotion, maybe?"

"Actually, the bonds have already been covered. Insurance is quick for somethin' like this."

Harmann scowled at the man for a long moment before abruptly snatching the bag off his shoulder and tossing it to Moore "Alright, numbnuts. You've done your job now beat it!"

The young man began to protest but Harmann took a threatening step towards him and he scurried away.

"Five minutes, Detective!" called the air traffic guy from nearby. He held a walkie talkie in his hand to speak with the tower and as he turned to stare down the runway, every eye followed his. Far in the distance, Harmann thought he could see the setting sun glinting off the wings of an aircraft, descending slowly.

"Come on you bastard." he muttered, a savage grin decorating his lips as he watched his prey approach.

CHAPTER 18

The jet coasted to a stop and was immediately the focus of more than a hundred rifle barrels. Furious, Harmann began yelling at anyone in earshot "Weapons down! Weapons down, goddamnit! This is a hostage situation, put your damn barrels down!"

Moore had been ready to walk forward but had stopped, understandably unwilling to walk into the convergence of so many itchy trigger fingers. As the gaggle of national guardsmen and police sheepishly lowered their barrels, she started forward.

"Door opening!" called a voice, unnecessarily as everyone could see the aft stairway being lowered with a hiss of hydraulics. A pale, nervous face appeared at the top of the steps and Moore raised a hand to indicate she was coming aboard. The figure beckoned before vanishing back into the cabin.

"Package going in." the running commentary crackled across the radios as Moore stepped onto the bottom step, gripping the handrail for balance.

"Package in."

Hope that ain't the last time I see that ass Harmann thought to himself as Moore vanished inside the cabin. Next to him, a stocky woman in the black windbreaker of SATA pressed a stopwatch and held it up for him to see.

"Ten seconds..."

He'd told Moore to be no more than a minute, but it was an arbitrary length of time. There was no plan B here. Well, he mused, that wasn't true but there was no plan B that didn't involve a lot of people dying as they stormed the aircraft. The SWAT commander stood nearby but his rifle was slung and his helmet off. His team were similarly unprepared. No-one wanted plan B to go into effect.

"Forty seconds..."

Goddamn! What was taking so long? Sweat ran down Harmann's back and he imagined Dunn's ugly face in the cabin, leering at Moore. He began second guessing himself. Should he have sent a male officer? Moore was too damn attractive to hope Dunn would simply let her go without at least trying to get her number. The cabin crew had said the man with had been charm itself to them, but Harmann knew it was all for show. Dunn was a killer and a savage and Harmann began kicking himself that he'd let Moore go unarmed into the monster's grasp.

"One minute, thirty seconds..."

"Sir?" the SWAT guy had moved closer. He didn't want to go in, but Harmann knew he would do it if it came down to it.

"Just wait..."

"Detective!" a shout made them all jump but it was the air traffic controller, radio still in his hand. He hurried over.

"What?" snapped Harmann.

"It's your partner..." he held the walkie out and Harmann snatched it up.

"This is Harmann."

"Detective? It's Moore. Sorry for the delay, he wanted to check the parachute." she sounded disappointed. Harmann had briefly considered messing with the 'chute they'd appropriated from a local skydiving school but had lacked the know-how to do this and it had been delivered by local law enforcement anyway, not an actual member of the school.

"Everything else alright?"

"Yes. I'm coming out now. The nine other passengers and the two cabin crew are coming too."

"Roger that." he turned to yell to the small army that was gathered around the plane "Hey! My officer plus the hostages are comin' out! We've got nine passengers plus two cabin crew! Keep your fingers off your damn triggers!" he was still furious at the way they'd reacted when the airplane had stopped. He gestured to the SWAT guy "They're yours."

The man nodded, finally clipping his helmet on and waving his team forward. They gathered in formation several feet back from the stairs as the empty space suddenly filled with Moore's red hair.

"Four minutes, forty eight seconds." the agent next to Harmann pushed the stop button and he nodded, staring as Moore came out, hands held out to the side. Next, came the passengers, a collection of frightened looking men and women, staring around in horror at the massed soldiers and cops surrounding them. The SWAT guy shouted his orders and the freed hostages obeyed as Moore approached Harmann.

"You okay?"

She nodded "Yeah. Captain is getting ready for take-off."

"Okay." Harmann grinned "Once they're wheels up, he's ours. Ain't no way Dunn is getting away!"

Moore did not smile "We've got a problem."

"What?"

"The guy with the bomb. He's black."

Harmann was suddenly aware of the agent with the stopwatch stiffening next to him. He'd barely noticed the fact that she too sported mahogany colored skin.

Moore shot her a withering glance as Harmann felt the blood drain from his face "Shit."

"What?" demanded the black woman, looking from Moore to Harmann. He did not respond, instead whipping out his cell and dialling Finnick.

Moore spared the agent a sympathetic look "Dunn is white. This guy ain't who we thought he was."

"Oh. Shit."

"Yup."

Behind them, the pilot hit the throttle and the jet began to roll along the runway, gathering speed. It leapt into the air and soon was lost in the pink hue of the setting sun.

CHAPTER 19

"Twenty million dollars? And we don't have anything apart from a damn e-fit?" Finnick's voice was distorted by interference on a bad line but Harmann did not need to concentrate to hear his boss yelling.

"Sir, it doesn't change anything. The Air Force are right with them and we've got helo's all across the state ready to get this sumbitch. Second he goes outta that plane, he's ours."

"Goddamnit, Harm! This means Dunn is still out there and you ain't got a lead on him! I'm telling you, Harm, you better get this guy on the ground!"

"We will, Sir. There's nothing he can do."

"Damn!" Finnick's voice was furious but his tone changed "The Director's here. Get this guy, Detective!"

"Sir -" but the line had gone dead and Harmann stared at his cell, tempted to toss it away. Instead, he pocketed it before climbing into the waiting airport branded SUV that carried him and Moore across to the tower. Inside, the glow of computer screens and the tinted glass allayed the bright light of the setting sun and without bothering to introduce himself, Harmann stalked over to a coffee machine and filled a styrofoam cup to the brim.

"Where are they?"

"Ten miles out, still climbing." replied a silver haired man with his back to Harmann.

"What height?"

"Nine thousand."

"Okay. How are our Air Force boys doin'?"

"They're with him."

"Alright."

"The hostages are debriefing." Moore had just hung up her own call.

"We're gonna need e-fits from each of them."

"They want to go home."

"I don't care. Get the e-fit. Then they can go to Mars for all I care."

Moore nodded and made a call.

Harmann sipped the coffee, which was weak and too hot, scalding his mouth. He cursed to himself, watching over the controller's shoulder at the radar blips.

"Anything from the Air Force?" he asked.

In response, the controller flipped a switch and the crackle of the Air Force pilots voices came over the radio.

"... Reached ten thousand feet. The aft door is open, looks like the pilot has hit the flaps to stabilise. Speed dropping a lot."

"Ask if they can see into the cabin." pestered Harmann and the controller sent the message.

"Negative. Cabin blinds are down. Cockpit is obscured by the light."

"Shit. What are they over now?"

The controller glanced at his maps "Um... Not much. Highways and scrubland out there. Basically into the desert."

"Any minute now then." Harmann reasoned and stood, tapping one foot on the floor as he waited for the Air Force pilots to make the call.

"Movement in the doorway."

"Here we go!" a grin shot across Harmann's face.

"Yup." if the controller was feeling the tension, he buried it deep "We got a black hawk from the 'guard right out there."

"Sweet!"

"We have visual on a falling body."

Harmann leaned forward, staring at the radar dots as though they would show him a live feed.

"'Chute sighted, I repeat, 'chute sighted. 'national tower, we are breaking off pursuit."

"Get the pilot!" Harmann shook the controller's shoulder.

"Which one?"

"The one in the jet! The one with the goddamn bomb aboard it!"

"Commercial two-three, this is 'national tower."

Static.

"Commercial two-three, this is 'national tower." The air traffic controller's voice was never anything less than calm as he repeated the call to the bomb laden jet.

"'National tower, this is Commercial two-three. Confirm suspect has left the aircraft. I repeat, the guy with the damn bomb has jumped out. Permission to return and land?"

"Commercial two-three, you are cleared to land, runway two, taxi alpha via alpha two. Whole place is yours."

"Roger 'national. Will call before finals. Commercial two-three out."

"Now the helo pilot!" shouted Harmann, unnecessarily as it turned out as the controller was already making the call.

"Guard four-two, Guard four-two this is 'national tower requesting sit-rep."

The voice of the national guard pilot came over the air in a fuzz of heavy static.

"Uuh - 'national tower this is Guard four-two with the national guard. We're about two minutes out."

"What? Who has eyes on the 'chute?" demanded Harmann, ice gripping his insides in a sudden panic.

The Air Force jets came back over before the controller could make the call.

"'Guard four-two this is Eagle six-eight, angels in the sky. Confirm my wingman and I have clear visual on the falling parachute."

Relief flooded through Harmann as he pulled out a vacant chair and collapsed into it "Whew! Goddamn I do not need another shock today." beside him, Moore gave a humourless smile, still watching over the controller's shoulder.

"'national tower this is Commercial two-three. Just to let you know we are making a wide loop around the area on our way back. Don't want to get in the way of our friends up here in the military."

"Was that the jet? The passenger one?" asked Harmann from his seat.

"Yup." the controller leaned forward "Commercial two-three, roger that last. Take your time, nobody rushing you home now."

Harmann could well imagine the shakes the flight crew were experiencing as the adrenaline left their systems and he nodded in sympathy at the controller's reassuring tone. He was confused, therefore by the controller's next words, spoken after a minute or two of silence.

"Uh. Commercial two-three, don't wanna backseat drive here but that's a mighty wide loop you're takin' there."

"What are they doing?" asked Harmann but Moore was pointing at the screen where the various dots were moving, their flight numbers standing out next to them.

"They're what, ten miles off course?"

The controller did not respond, instead keying his mic "Commercial two-three, Commercial two-three, this is 'national tower, radio check, over."

Static.

Frowning, the controller shot a look at Harmann before making another call.

"Eagle six-eight, Eagle six-eight, this is 'national tower. Do you have a visual on Commercial two-three?"

"Uuh that's a negative, 'national tower. We've got all our eyes on this sucker in the 'chute. He's just about on the ground right now."

"Could you take a detour and pick up Commercial two-three? We're not able to establish contact."

"Roger that. On our way."

"Uuh 'national tower this is Guard four-two. We're just touchin' down by the suspect. Gimme a minute and you'll have a good sitrep."

"Come on..." Harmann had leaned forward, elbows on his

knees and both hands clenched into fists in front of his mouth as though he were watching the tense final play in a game.

"'national tower, this is Guard four-two. We've got a man in our custody here but he's the first officer from that jet. Presume your bomber is still aboard."

"Ethnicity! Get his damn ethnicity!" snapped Harmann, leaping up and clapping the controller on the shoulder.

"Uh - Guard four-two from 'national tower, could you confirm the detainee's skin color?"

"Sure. This guy's whiter than Abe Lincoln."

The controller was already calling "Eagle six-eight, we need a visual on that jet, stat. What can you tell us?"

"Nothing here... Wait, got 'em. We have visual on the jet, heading towards you at eight thousand feet. Back door is still open."

A sudden burst of static and a panicked voice came over the radio,

"'National tower, Air Force boys, anyone who's fucking listening this is Commercial two-three heading your way as fast as I can go. Listen - the guy with the bomb jumped out about five minutes ago. He's left the damn package in my cabin, told me there was a timer on it. He made my first officer jump out and told me to call and say that was him. I repeat, he left my aircraft about five minutes ago and said to wait that long before I called you. Please God say you've got a bomb disposal guy waiting for me down there!"

Anything else that was said was lost as Harmann flung the half-drunk coffee across the control tower and booted the swivel chair into the nearest row of monitors.

"Fuck!"

Moore was staring open mouthed at the controller's back, struggling to comprehend the turn of events. The jet pilot was reporting back as he searched the sky for a second parachute.

"How the fuck were there two parachutes?" Harmann demanded, furiously. He rounded on Moore, half tempted to slap the stupid expression off her face "How many did you take?"

"One. Just one! You gave me the damn thing!"

"Then how were there two? How!" he roared this last word as the elevator binged behind them and the door opened to admit a pair of airport police, flanking the insurance guy from the airline.

"I heard on the walkie talkie-" he gestured lamely out the windows "I thought you guys knew about the second 'chute?"

Harmann crossed the tower floor in a single leaping stride, grabbing the younger man by the lapels and ramming him back into the wall.

"No! I did not know about the fucking second parachute! Why didn't you tell us? Huh?"

Two pairs of hands seized him, hauling him backwards.

"Take it easy, Detective!"

"Yeah, give the guy a break!"

"Get the fuck off me! Damn rent-a-cops!" spat Harmann but he stepped back from the two airport cops. Against the wall, the insurance guy was panting, his face filled with fury.

"As it happens, Detective -" he laboured the word, sarcastically as he straightened his suit "I was gonna tell you but you told me to beat it, remember?"

Harmann's hand twitched towards his gun and for a moment he thought he might actually draw it and shoot the young man right there in the tower but instead, sense prevailed.

"If you'd taken the time to listen to me, I'd have said that the aircraft is designed for skydiving! We do a package - a luxury package for our clients to sip champagne and eat caviar before they jump. There are always 'chutes on the plane. But you'da thunk a smart guy like you would know that." he shot Harmann a look of pure malice and turned, stalking into the elevator.

"Motherfucker!" shouted Harmann but the doors had binged shut and there was no-one to vent his rage on. He stood, fists balled by his sides as the airport cops shuffled nervously, unsure what to do now.

"How the fuck did we miss this?" asked Moore in a furious hiss.

Harmann did not trust himself to speak. Instead, he closed his eyes, swallowing hard and forced himself to breathe, to think, to detect. Behind him, the jets were combing the ground and a second flight of national guard choppers was on the move, six of them.

"We'll find him. We've still got the initiative. We've got F-35's and helos. Motherfucker is ours!" Harmann told himself over and over again but nothing, not the confident voices on the radio nor the words in his head could remove the terrible sinking feeling gnawing at the pit of his stomach.

In his mind's eye, a single, lonely parachute drifted to earth, a faceless man suspended beneath it, laughing his ass off as twenty million dollars in untraceable bearer bonds rested safely in his hands.

Harmann's phone rang.

It was Finnick.

He didn't even have the energy to defend himself as he answered the call and waited for the executioner's axe to swing.

CHAPTER 20

"I simply do not have the words, Detective."

The director of SATA had never been Harmann's friend. A political appointment, the day to day running of the agency was left to Finnick but today, Barbara Soames had taken the time to descend from her lofty world of fundraisers and board meetings to do her level best to stamp out the last of Harmann's self-respect.

"Yes, ma'am."

"Do you have anything to say for yourself?"

"I've said everything in my report, ma'am."

Soames pulled the paper towards her on the highly polished mahogany of Finnick's desk although she had already sat and read it whilst Harmann stood awkwardly in front of her. Finnick stood to one side, his usual spot temporarily surrendered to his boss.

"A report where you blame everyone except yourself, I note." Soames looked up at him, steel in her eyes "If it weren't for your already exemplary record, Detective, you'd be handing over your badge and gun right now."

"Yes, ma'am."

"As it happens, your young partner may well have to take the fall for this."

Beside him, Harmann felt Moore stir in shock and what little part of him still cared about such things rose to the forefront "Ma'am, if I may, Probationary Detective Moore has behaved in an professional fashion throughout the investigation. As you'll see from my report, she volunteered to walk unarmed into that aircraft to ensure the instructions were carried out to the letter.

I don't wish to make excuses, ma'am, but I fail to see how any other officer would've dealt with the situation more effectively."

And let that keep your mouth shut, bitch he thought bitterly, praying his words in her defense would stop Moore from telling Soames about the insurance guy and the little titbit of information that had changed the course of this case. He'd left it out of the wording of his report, filling in the gaps with some interesting interpretations of the truth but Moore had been silent since they'd finally left the control tower as the search was called off and he'd wondered if she was going to throw him under the bus.

Soames fixed Moore with her best death stare "Do you agree with this report, Moore?"

Harmann held his breath, but he needn't have worried.

"Yes, ma'am. I don't see any other way we could've done it. Neither does anyone else in the agency."

Harmann resisted the urge to grin. Soames was an outspoken feminist, bullying the agency to fill diversity quotas, recruiting dozens of women and fast tracking them to senior positions and he knew that Moore's words were worth a thousand of his.

Soames looked a shade less steely at Moore's declaration and she blinked several times.

"Well. That's as may be. I appreciate your candour, Moore. How long do you have left in your probation?"

"Six months, ma'am. Detective Harmann is my signatory."

"Perhaps you can speed that process up a little, Harmann?"

"It'd be my pleasure, ma'am." he lied *Fucking she-fag* he thought, silently.

"Detective - detectives - I am going to give you one last chance." Soames laid her carefully manicured nails flat on the report, staring at both of them "I want this man, this terrorist found and I want to see him in court. Without that, someone in the agency is going to have to take the fall and I can assure you that it will not be me, nor Deputy Director Finnick. That leaves you, Detective."

"Yes, ma'am."

"Find him, Detective."
"Yes, ma'am."

CHAPTER 21

"Thanks, Moore. I owe ya one."

They were in Harmann's office, a self-congratulatory chamber covered in newspaper clippings of successful arrests. The stars and stripes hung beside the window opposite a state flag whilst on the desk, Harmann had framed his college degree next to a smartly mounted bowie knife engraved with a message of thanks from the mayor of the state capital.

If he expected Moore to smile and pass it off, he was disappointed. Instead, she cut straight to the chase.

"What do we know about this guy?"

Harmann sighed, removing his jacket and tossing it onto his chair where the various objects inside clicked and pinged. He leaned on the windowsill, staring down at the street ten storeys below.

"Black, thirty to fifty, charming, fit and healthy, knows how to jump out of a plane and not die, moves like a goddamn ghost on the ground, knows how to make a bomb." he shook his head.

"The bomb was a dud." Moore reminded him "They said it was a good dud, but there was no actual explosive material. Everything else worked though, from the timers to the power source. The only way we know it wasn't the genuine article is your pal Gilruth tested the explosive and realised it was fake."

"Damn." Harmann considered "Alright. It's a pretty tight skillset. Presume he has a skydiving background and that's how he knew about the jet. Then he had to know about the D. B. Cooper case -"

"Everyone knows about that. It's famous. It's on Wikipedia for God's sake."

"Okay." Harmann conceded the point "But since then, they put controls in place on commercial airliners so you can't safely open the doors and jump out. It's to stop stuff like this. That's why the guy surrendered last time. He didn't know that and I showed him."

Moore frowned "I thought you pulled your gun on him? That's what the after action report said. I wrote about it."

Harmann shot her a disgusted look "Finnick knew the truth. Reports get glamourized, it helps the agency look good. And I did draw my gun, as it happened. Come on, concentrate." he pulled out his chair "What type of people have that sort of skill set?"

"Military."

"I think that's pretty obvious. Don't SEAL's train like this?"

"Sure. Ranger's do too. Green berets, pararescue, airborne. There's probably a few thousand guys right now in the country who could pull this off no problem."

"Okay... But it still gives us a narrower pool."

"Right. But we start sending this e-fit out, might be they go to ground. Military guys are tight."

"Sure, but if we-"

The landline on Harmann's desk rang. Frowning at the withheld number he picked it up.

"Harmann." he listened for a second then muttered "Hang on." before pushing the speaker button and replacing the handset. Moore leaned closer, eyes narrowing at the sobs emanating from the receiver.

"Say that again, ma'am." Harmann asked and the female voice on the other end of the phone choked on a sob before speaking again.

"I said, my husband was the one who done that airplane jacking. I saw it on the news. I got proof."

Harmann stared at Moore, seeing the shock he felt reflected on her face.

"What's your name, ma'am?"

"Yvonne Brooke. I live at 135, New Hampton way." she read off a zip code and Harmann hastened to scribble it down.

"Ma'am, my partner and I are on our way over to you now. Is your husband home?"

"No, but I can show you where he is."

"What's his name?"

"Huh?"

"Your husband. What's his name?"

"Oh. It's Charlie. Charlie Brooke."

Harmann hung up and shot Moore a look of pure joy.

"Got the bastard."

CHAPTER 22

The Brooke' address was in a shit-heap town called Ranger, an hours drive away. Red brick roads lay between low, wood faced, single story shacks that barely qualified as liveable. The sun had reached its peak and there wasn't a scrap of shade within the town limits and Harmann resisted the urge to sneer as they made their way along the wide roads.

"Here..."

A dilapidated building lacking any kind of perimeter fence baked in the sun. A rusted pickup, standing on bricks instead of wheels stood in the front yard surrounded by engine parts, all of them baked by the scalding sun. Opposite, an ugly brown brick building, erupting out of the yellowish, brownish dirt that covered the town, bore the legend 'BROOKE TACTICAL'. A 'closed' sign hung in the door.

"Brooke... Goddamn. Guy owns the gun store." Harmann glanced through his sunglasses at Moore who shrugged.

"She said he wasn't home."

"Best hope she was right. Still." Harmann drew his piece and racked the slide as quietly as he could. Holding the pistol down at his side, he pointed and Moore, echoing his drawn weapon, shifted to the side of the barely visible dirt track that led to the front door.

"Round the back?" Moore suggested but Harmann shook his head, trusting his gut.

He knocked.

Silence. Then from inside the house, the sound of steady footsteps and the inner door opened, leaving the screen door intact.

"Is that you? The cops?"

Harmann moved into view "Mrs Brooke?"

"Yes!" she pushed the door open, revealing a white woman with puffy red eyes.

"Is your husband home?"

"No! He ain't here, I can promise you that."

With a significant look at Moore, Harmann stepped in, the Glock still in his hand. He unceremoniously pushed Mrs Brooke aside, moving silently with Moore to clear the low building. It was empty. It was also stiflingly hot inside.

"Where is your husband, ma'am?" he asked as he holstered the Glock.

"He's -" she choked back a sob "He's with his goddamn whore!" she spat the last word out with pure venom as though it were the worst sentence she could bestow upon a fellow human being.

"Maybe you could explain, ma'am?" Moore spoke softly, taking the lady by the elbow and directing her to a dirty, overstuffed armchair in what qualified as the living room.

Yvonne Brooke sagged into the chair and reached a well-practiced hand to a box of kleenex balancing on the arm. She was overcome by sobs and gestured at an open laptop resting atop a pile of old magazines on a rickety looking coffee table. Moore nodded to it and Harmann stepped forward, gingerly tugging his tactical pen from his lapel.

On the screen, something close to a homemade porno had been paused. Frozen in mid action, a muscular looking black man was apparently in the midst of vigorously thrusting into a skinny looking white woman who, although Harmann could not make out her face from this angle, did not appear to be Mrs Brooke. He narrowed his eyes, leaning closer.

" That ain't you?" Mrs Brooke shook her head "What a freakin' moron." Harmann shook his head, tapping the spacebar with the end of the pen. The figures on the screen resumed their frantic copulating with a series of moans and gasps that would've made the internet blush.

Moore reached over and tapped the pause button as Mrs

Brooke's sobs rose into a fever pitch "Ma'am? Do you know who this woman is?"

Yvonne shook her head, sniffing angrily "No. I don't know her name but I saw my husband with her in the gun store."

"Does he own the gun store, Ma'am?" Harmann asked and the woman nodded, a fresh wave of hysteria gripping her.

Leaving Moore to ply her womanly comforts, Harmann stepped away, examining the small dwelling at a slower pace than he had. His eye rested on a prominent photo showing a smiling black man, almost identical to the e-fit of their bomber standing with a group of servicemen, the unmistakable badge of the Ranger Regiment above them.

"Was your husband in the military, ma'am?" he called back.

"Y - yes. Army Rangers. He got out about ten years back. Never been the same since." Yvonne began sobbing again.

"Ma'am." Harmann had scooped the photo up and pocketed it "We need to find your husband. Right now."

She nodded, dragging the laptop towards her and closing the adulterous video. She pulled up a search engine and entered an address, bringing up the interactive map.

"Here..." she pointed to a building in the next town over.

"He's in the bar?" Harmann was suspicious.

"'Course he is. That's where he always is. Drunk as anythin'. That's where his whore is from. Goddamn bitch. I don't care if you shoot 'em both."

Harmann did not spare Mrs Brookes another thought. Leaving Moore with the woman, he raced out to the car, firing the ignition and spinning the wheel whilst he called it in.

"Yes, full assault team. I'm taking no chances! Sure, call the sheriff. Call the fire department, the pre-school teachers and the city council if you want. This motherfucker is going down!"

CHAPTER 23

Ray was up a ladder fixing the fan which had stopped without warning an hour ago. Tom leaned around the old Navajo's frame, trying to still see the TV.

"You done yet?" he asked for the fiftieth time.

"Nope."

Darell approached the bar and leaned over, helping himself to four more cold beers which he clinked together meaningfully. Ray glanced down and nodded once before turning back to the fan.

A voice, neither Tom's nor Ray's rose in sudden emotion, drawing everyone's attention with a nervous energy. All eyes rested on the booth behind Tom's normal perch where three men had been huddled in a heart-to-heart that brooked no interruption. Not for the first time, Tom felt the urge to stalk over there, to bully the sour faced man who dominated the exchange but a potent sense of self preservation kept his butt firmly on the bar stool. Instead, he knocked back another shot and tried to distract himself by bothering Ray.

"You need a new fuse?" Tom asked.

"I need you ta stop hollerin' at me."

"How 'bout -"

The door flew in with a crash. Suddenly, the humid air was filled with a press of bodies, waving guns and shouting commands. Tom was just drunk enough that he paused before reaching for his revolver and so the two lead guys dressed in the uniforms of the Sherriff's office were able to grab him and wrestle him to the floor before he could complete his bad decision.

"Hey! Git the hell offa me -" Tom yelled as they twisted his arm behind his back.

"Get him off that ladder!"

A crash and a yell announced Ray being tugged from his perch.

"You! Hands on the wall!"

Tom heard Darell protest with the irritating stubbornness borne only of being an old, drunk southern white man.

"Git!"

Shouted recriminations, then a single voice, local accent saying in a clear, calm tone "Where is Charlie Brookes?"

"You ain't gettin' Charlie!" roared Tom before someone kneed him in the side of the head and he decided to keep quiet.

"I'll ask one more time!" the voice threatened "Where is Charlie Brookes?"

"Here."

The response was quiet, measured and calm. All eyes, including Tom's, turned to the booth where the big black man had stood up. Without a glance at his companions, the surly faced man and a smaller, skinny looking Asian, he stepped clear of the booth and, with a slowness that belied a terrible patience and never taking his eyes from the Detective, he raised his hands to his head, interlacing the fingers and dropped with a bone jarring thud to his knees.

Everyone was still for a moment. Tom held his breath.

Then the spell was broken as three officers hurried over, throwing Charlie unnecessarily to the floor, bouncing his face off the floorboards as they wrestled his hands behind his back.

The Detective stepped aside, letting the uniformed officers wrestle on the dirty floor. Instead, his eyes turned to the small booth where the surly man was glaring up at Harmann with dark eyes. He made no move to fight, no attempt to resist the inevitable. Instead, he turned his head slightly to the side, as though curious to see how this unexpected turn of events would play out.

More officers descended on him at Harmann's instruction,

cuffing him roughly alongside the skinny man who had made to stand up but instead had stumbled and was now wide eyed with fear. He stated up at Harmann as though he were the executioner, waiting to pounce. Instead of a death blow, however, the Detective stowed his weapon, pulling a cell phone from his pocket and tapping a contact.

"Sir? Yeah. We got him. And guess who his drinking buddy was?" Harmann grinned his toothy beam of victory at the surly man "You'll never guess it, Sir. One William C. Dunn. Trussed like a turkey."

CHAPTER 24

"Well, Sir, Moore got the information out of the wife. The lady was hysterical and it took a calm hand for sure."

Moore blinked in surprise. It wasn't the first time this afternoon. Harmann stood opposite her, cell to his ear as he gave his initial report to Finnick. This surprise was because she hadn't expected credit from the Detective but she dipped her head in acknowledgement. Mrs Brooke had been hysterical for sure but even as Harmann had been kicking in the door of Ray's bar the woman had been spilling details of her husband's crimes like a faucet ripped off a sink.

"Yes, Sir. I'll be sure to pass that on to her. Yes. I'll call you after the interrogations, Sir." he hung up and shot a sly grin at Moore.

"Director is pretty damn happy with you. She's gonna sign your probation off personally."

Moore nodded "Thanks."

Harmann shook his head "Nope, ain't me that needs thankin'. Without you, we'd 'a lost the other two. Now we got the whole gang." his teeth flashed as they turned back to the bank of monitors in the basement control room. Most were dark but the glow from three drew their eyes as the prisoners sat baking in the ninety degree heat.

"Who we gonna hit first?"

"Dunn." Harmann clenched his fists "I wanna look this motherfucker in the eye."

"He's got his lawyer."

"So? Lawyer ain't gettin' him outta this. We got him."

"Think he'll confess?"

"Nope. I think he'll sit there and say nuthin'. C'mon."

Harmann pushed the control room door open and stepped out into the neon lit corridor. The seal and motto of the SATA was emblazoned on every door along with bold printed warnings reading 'CHECK YOUR WEAPON' and 'CRIME DOESN'T PAY'. Harmann paused outside the heavy door almost directly opposite and paused, giving Moore a nod. He shoved the door open.

Instantly, Dunn's lawyer was on his feet, his shirt padded with sweat patches and indignation on his brow "This is illegal! You must turn the AC on, or I demand you move my client to a new interrogation room!"

Harmann affected a frown, glancing in confusion at the silent air conditioner "Oh? Is it not working?" he made a great show of stepping over and rapping smartly on it with his knuckles. As if by magic, the vents slid open and a wave of cool air flooded the small room. Harmann turned his white smile on the lawyer and his stony-faced client who was handcuffed to the D-ring on the metal table "See? All workin'."

"You must move my client to another room -" began the lawyer, a state appointed attorney.

"Why? AC's workin'. Maybe you coulda just given it a knock yourself?" he grinned hugely. Both men knew that the AC had been turned off intentionally and Harmann's sham had been just that but the lawyer also knew he could prove nothing and so he sat down with a scowl, enjoying the cool breeze.

Harmann spoke loudly for the record "William C. Dunn, arrested for... Let me see." he made a great show of flipping through the paperwork on the desk before him "Attempted murder, robbery, armed robbery times four, grand theft auto, grand larceny... Oh, and indecent exposure." that last one made Harmann smile and he looked Dunn in the eyes "Really? You're a piece of work, Dunn, but I ain't had you as a pervert."

"My client proposes a plea deal -" began the lawyer "- he will plead guilty to the armed robbery charges if you'll drop the attempted murder charges-"

"No! No, no, no, no." Harmann leaned forward "See, I think

your client knows that he ain't ever gonna see the light of day as a free man here. We got him with Deee Ennn Ayyy -" he dragged the three syllables out "- on attempted murder of two state officials." this time the grin on his lips was truly evil "That's two capital offences, Dunn. They gon' hang you, you evil motherfucker."

"My client has not been convicted of anything! He-"

"Aw, shut the hell up, wouldya?" Harmann snapped "Look, I've already won here. Dunn, you ain't gettin' out but I tell you what. You wanna plea deal? Here it is. We'll drop the attempted murder if you plead guilty to the armed robbery charges."

The lawyer began to nod but Harmann held up a hand "I ain't finished. Armed robbery - that's five counts, Dunn. Fifty to life if I'm any judge." he laughed at the joke "And you gotta plead guilty to the indecent exposure charge." Harmann sat back.

"You don't have any evidence for that charge-" the lawyer protested and in response, Harmann turned the stack of papers around mutely and pushed it across the table. The lawyer seized it greedily, poring over the case notes. Harmann saw his eyes widen and he shot Dunn a glance. The rugged criminal remained stony faced, hands relaxed on the desk and his gaze on Harmann.

Who stood up, slapping both hands on the table and making the attorney jump "That's the deal. Attempted murder times two and a noose or all the others and you go down as a sex criminal. It's your life, Dunn." Harmann nodded to Moore and they left the cell, slamming the heavy door behind them.

"Whew!" Harmann was grinning like a kid on Christmas. Moore was looking quietly impressed and she nodded at his exultation.

"Are those deals agreed by the director?"

"Sure. Look, we gave him two shitty choices there but you know what? I think he'll go for the capital crimes. Dunn is about forty and it'll be ten years before he sees a noose. I reckon ten years on death row is better in anyone's mind than another forty or fifty bein' run through in the showers every day." Harmann shrugged "'Course, I'd have loved to put a bullet in the guy but this is good enough."

"I take it he didn't have a weapon?"

"Nope. Shame." Harmann shrugged again "Maybe he'll go for a firing squad when they convict him and I can volunteer to pull the trigger. Don't matter now."

Moore felt she should offer some words of congratulations. After all, Dunn was one of the most violent men in the state and he was now going away for the rest of his life but Harmann had already moved on down the corridor.

"Go for the boss next?"

"Nah, I want to see this guy we don't know. This -" Harmann checked the name on the digital screen outside the interrogation room "- Singh. Mohsin Singh." he pushed the handle.

Mohsin Singh was a skinny twenty something with nut brown skin. His eyes were black and danced nervously from Harmann to Moore, coming to rest on her flawless features.

"Wha'cha lookin' at, boy?" snapped Harmann and Singh's eyes widened in fear and locked on the tall Detective as he pulled out a chair and lowered himself into it without breaking eye contact.

"I- I don't mean -"

"Stop yammerin'." Harmann knew it was key to keep the initiative in these kinds of interviews. The young man had no record, had never been arrested and hadn't even known to ask for a lawyer. Until he thought of that, Harmann had to keep him on the backfoot and get a confession out of him. Moore could play good cop, he thought, judging by the way Singh was looking at her.

"We got you for money launderin', armed robbery, illegal possession of a firearm, resistin' arrest and any other charge we care to slap on ya." Harmann watched the eyes widen and the fists clench.

"I didn't mean to resist! I fell off my chair -"

"You resisted! I saw it myself! We got it all on body worn video, too." that was a lie, Harmann didn't think any of the sheriff's deputies he'd commandeered had ever even heard of a body cam but he knew he could pass it off as a mistake if a lawyer picked it up later.

"No! You've got it all wrong-"

Harmann slapped his palm on the table, cupping it just slightly so the sound was maximised and cracked like a gunshot through the small room. Singh jumped back in his chair, the handcuffs going taught.

"You got one good choice to make here, boy." Harmann had leaned forward, his eyes boring holes in Singh's face "You tell us what you did, how you did it, where the money went and then I'll see about gettin' you a plea deal." the flash of hope in Singh's eyes was just what he'd expected and he squashed it like a fly against a wall "If you don't, we're lookin' at fifty to life. Most likely life for you." he embellished although he knew that wasn't true.

"I never had a firearm! I don't like guns-"

"You don't like guns? In this state? Goddamn, boy! You ain't gettin' yourself into my good graces here!"

A thought occurred to Harmann and he narrowed his eyes, squinting at the man as though he were a hundred yards away, not just the other side of the table "Do I know you? I think I know your face."

"I - I've never met you before." stammered the man.

"Look, just tell us what you know." Moore had leaned forward as Harmann had leaned backwards, her voice gently but insistent. Harmann had to resist the urge to clap his hands at the smoothness of it all, as though they'd choreographed the routine perfectly.

She laid it on thick as Harmann affected an exasperated look "We can help you out here, Mohsin. We know you aren't the big bad here. You're the clever one who got in with the wrong crowd."

Had she actually just winked at him? Harmann would have to check the surveillance footage later.

"Let's start with a couple'a easy ones, huh? My name's Detective Moore. Jeanne Moore. I'm an investigator with the SATA. What's your name?"

Christ! Sounds like they're on a date! Harmann had to work to keep his features straight. Right now, he'd never been more attracted to Moore and he inhaled, enjoying the faint whiff of her perfume.

"I - my name is Mohsin Singh. Mo. I'm an accountant."

"Where you from, Mo?"

"Minnesota."

"That's a helluva way from here." Moore affected surprise, managing to convey at the same time that the young man being a long way from home was somehow impressive.

Mohsin nodded at the implied compliment "Yeah. Been here four years now."

"You like it here?"

"Sure. Weather's great. People are nice, too." he smiled at her.

"Yeah. We sure are friendly down here."

You damn southern belle Harmann thought.

"How'd you find gettin' work down here?"

"Alright. Plenty of people need their taxes doing." Mohsin shrugged and smiled as though he were not cuffed to a metal table in a sunless basement.

"I hear ya. Maybe you can do mine some time."

Goddamn keep talkin' like that, sweet little thang! Harmann thought he might cream his pants.

Mohsin apparently thought the same because he smiled and nodded.

"Before we do that, you gotta tell us a couple'a things though." her voice turned serious although still friendly. She'd leaned forward, clearly flashing some cleavage to Mohsin.

"I can do that."

"These robberies..." she actually trailed a fingertip across the table.

Mohsin swallowed, glanced at her chest then nodded "I - I was the accountant. I - I moved the money for them."

"Who were 'they'?" Harmann cut across harshly.

Mohsin jumped, stammering "I - Charlie and Will."

"Charlie and Will? Gotta be more specific than that, boy."

"Charlie Brooke and William Dunn."

"They did the robberies with you?"

"Yes."

"Who did what?"

"Dunn told us when and where. Dunn had the gun. I showed Charlie how to hack those machines."

"Then what?"

"Then I pushed it through the system. Laundered it."

"You laundered all of it?"

"Yeah. Every bit."

"You're gonna need to tell us how." Harmann had lowered his voice.

Mohsin shook his head.

Harmann stared.

"I mean - I don't know. You gotta ask Dunn for that."

"Bullshit."

The conversation ground to a frosty halt. Mohsin suddenly looked terrified again.

"You mean to tell me that Dunn knows where the money is and you - the accountant - don't?" Harmann did not need to fake his anger.

"I know a couple of bits but no - he had all the details of where it was going. I -"

"What bits?"

"I -"

"Mo, how about you write it all down for us, huh?" Moore cut across Harmann and he let her. She pushed a pencil and a blank sheet of paper across the table "I can tell you want to help and we aren't making you feel very welcome." she phrased it as an apology and Mohsin actually looked contrite, like he wanted to apologise to her!

"I'll do it - I'll write it down but Dunn knows all the account details and numbers. He wouldn't tell me-"

"It's okay, Mo." she'd actually put a hand on his as they both stood up "We're gonna go have a little talk with Charlie and then I'll come back in a bit and we can have us a heart to heart."

97

The poor accountant nodded like one of those dogs people stuck on their dash. Harmann ducked for the door, he couldn't trust his face anymore. Moore smiled at Mohsin as she shut the door, turning to Harmann who clapped his hands at her.

"Goddamn, you're good, Moore! Goddamn!"

"Thanks."

"Alright. Strike whilst the iron's hot?"

"Sure."

Harmann lead the way into the third room, reading the name on the digital screen 'Charlie Brooke'.

CHAPTER 25

Harmann had practiced his game face for decades. Every moment of entering an interrogation room for the first time was a practiced, well-oiled routine that he'd measured and adjusted a thousand times. Inevitably, the factor in constant flux was the reaction of the perp on the other side of the door. Over the years he'd seen every emotion from drugged out schitzoid to resigned grief. Some laughed bravely, some wept pitifully and others raged and threatened, vowing to fight the system to their dying breath.

Once people were arrested, they ceased to be a threat in Harmann's eyes. Once he'd got them, the system had them and he knew it did not release its prisoners easily. The handcuffs may be the physical restraint but the invisible looming presence of the courtroom, the jail cells and tall walls formed just as much of a barrier as the steel rings.

He was shocked, then, when he strode into the room, ignoring the relaxed looking lawyer who'd thought to bring a pair of small battery operated hand fans to keep him and his client cool, to see Charlie Brooke's eyes, locking onto him with all the accuracy of a laser guided missile system and conveying through their glassy darkness the most profoundly disturbing look of utter human disgust that he'd ever come across.

It struck Harmann, causing him to falter in his step. He missed a beat and as a consequence, every other motion seemed to lose its cohesion. He pulled the left hand of the two chairs out, snagging the foot on the metal table leg with a muted clang that drew every eye. Then he sat down too heavily, aware of the thump his ass made on the hard polymer. Moore sat down smoothly next to him and Harmann became aware that he'd pulled the chair too far back, that Moore had her elbows on the table whereas he was almost a foot from it. Hastening to correct himself, he gripped the sides of the chair with his hands and shuffled it forwards, the feet grating on the hard floor. Unbidden into his mind came the image of a naughty child, shuffling his own seat in a school auditorium and as he glanced up into the amused face of the lawyer, Harmann flushed with fury.

"Alright!" his voice was too loud. Moore twitched in response as the lawyer's face grew more amused.

"Charlie Brooke. We've got you for-"

"Ain't you that cop that murdered that old lady?"

Harmann stared stupidly at the lawyer before realising the man hadn't spoken, that his client had uttered the words. He looked at Charlie who stared back at him with eyes that were a terrible jet black. The white's themselves were flecked with darkness and the lids above and below were creased beyond the man's years, the upper lid slightly lower than it should be giving a disarming stillness to his gaze.

Harmann was flustered but he had been a cop for three decades and he recovered himself quickly, ignoring the outburst "We've got you for armed robbery, attempted murder, conspiracy to wilfully cause destruction of an aircraft - which could be a federal crime -"

"It was you. You was the one that killed that old lady." Charlie sat back, the handcuffs clinking. His arms remained on the table and Harmann realised in that moment just how big the black man was. Well over six feet and set with lean muscle mass, belying the years of drinking his wife said he'd experienced.

"My client is not being charged with attempted murder." interjected the lawyer "Nor can you prove conspiracy to wilfully cause destruction of an aircraft."

"We can-"

"That's a federal crime and you ain't a Fed." the lawyer made it sound like an insult.

Harmann was on the back foot and he knew it. He sought

desperately to regain his cool, even flicking a glance at Moore but she was frozen, unable to take her lead from him.

Harmann paused for a moment, letting his gaze rest on the lawyer and allowing the break to let the sentence form on his tongue "Armed robbery. Attempted murder. Conspiracy to destroy."

"No."

Charlie spoke and all eyes turned to him. His own gaze never left Harmann.

"I ain't conspired to destroy. There weren't no explosive in that suitcase. Nor did I hurt anyone. You hurt anyone lately, Detective?"

Harmann had the odd feeling that Charlie's eyes were x-raying him. He shifted minutely on the hard chair, wishing Moore would say something "We ain't here to talk about me." it was the wrong thing to say. It made him sound guilty even to his own lips. Unbidden, the face of Mavis Delayney came into his mind. Not the smiling photo that had been released to the press, but the terrible staring dead eyes of an innocent woman in the wrong place at the wrong time.

Harmann changed tack "Let's talk about your military record. You were an army Ranger, right?"

"I don't see how that's relevant." protested the lawyer.

"It's relevant, Sir, because this man hijacked a damn airplane with a bomb! He caused two Air Force jets to pull away and track the aircraft at great expense to the taxpayer and a whole company from the national guard to go chasin' around the damn desert lookin' for him for days!"

"That isn't my client's fault."

"The hell it ain't his fault! Whose fault is it then?"

"My client cannot be held responsible for the deployment of the military in this circumstance. He left the service ten years ago."

"So, you were in the Rangers." Harmann saw the flash of annoyance in the lawyer's eye and grinned at the small victory, feeling more in control "How many jumps did you do?"

"That's not -"

"More'n you had hot dinners." grated Charlie and Harmann looked at the man, instantly regretting it. The hatred and disgust was plain to see.

"What the fuck is your problem with me?" demanded Harmann, suddenly losing it. He rose to his feet "You got somethin' to say to me, boy, you better come out and say it!"

Charlie regarded him with that same expression. Harmann was about to make a dismissive sound when Charlie spoke "Easy for you to say when you got me cuffed to a table. What I got to say ain't right to do with words."

"The fuck is that s'posed to mean?"

"You a smart guy. You figure it out."

Charlie turned to Moore, sitting opposite him "Detective Moore, ain't it? It's good to see you again." he smiled, the ice cold mask vanishing in an instant.

"I wish I could say the same." Moore sounded uncertain.

"I just wanted to take the time to say thank you for your good manners in the cabin of that airplane." Charlie's smile was so genuine and warm it made Harmann shiver at the contrast in the big man's manner "You really did help to smooth all them things over. I'm sorry we had to meet under them circumstances."

"You wanna keep talkin' to her like that?" Harmann was still standing "Maybe you think that's another time you can cheat on your wife?" He watched for a reaction in the former Ranger but instead the lawyer leapt to his feet.

"Now wait just a damn minute!" he pointed a finger at the Detective "That is not your business. What my client does in his personal life has nothing to do with his arrest! You, Detective, are here to ask your questions then be on your damn way!"

"Oh, is that right?" Harmann rounded on the lawyer, seeing the man flinch.

"It was you! You shot that old lady in the bank robbery." Charlie interjected as Harmann felt another level of self-control vanish as he rounded on the handcuffed man.

Moore leapt to her feet, hands held out to both of them "Let's take a damn minute here, huh?" when Harmann didn't move, she cocked her head at him in a pleading gesture. He sat down and a moment later, the lawyer followed suit.

Moore took over "Can you confirm where you were on..." she began scanning the documents, looking for the date of the crime.

"I was in that airplane, as you know." Charlie spoke calmly.

"So, you admit it?" Harmann shot across the table.

"Sure."

"My client has always intended to plead guilty." put in the lawyer.

Moore looked confused and Harmann was shocked "Then why are we havin' this damn hootenanny?" he demanded "Guilty! We'll get you in front of the judge by mornin'!"

"Oh, no. My client intends to plead guilty to assisting in an armed robbery."

"What? No. He planned the whole thing! We know he did!"

"No, you don't." the lawyer said this flatly and Harmann felt the words fall like a lead weight on the room. He considered the proof they had for the bank robberies. Basically zip.

"Look, listen for just one moment, Detective." the lawyer leaned forward, his face now earnest "My client has committed crimes, he accepts his punishment for that, but we have recorded evidence that he was coerced into these by William C. Dunn. Mr Dunn threatened my client's life, his business and his wife and so Mr Brooke had no choice but to go along with it."

"That's bullshit!" snapped Harmann but Moore leaned forward.

"Why didn't he report Mr Dunn to law enforcement?"

"Mr Brooke was preparing to hand over all the evidence he'd collated. In fact - " the lawyer scooped his ornate leather briefcase from the floor and opened it on the desk, removing a plastic evidence bag filled with flash drives "These are recordings Mr Brooke made of his interactions with Mr Dunn and you will see clearly that Mr Dunn blackmailed my client into committing these actions. This is why Mr Brooke contacted me before his arrest and made me aware of these circumstances."

Harmann stared at the drives in dismay. Moore pulled the bag towards her "We'll need to verify these. Mr Brooke, how did you manage to make these recordings? It must have taken some technical know-how."

Charlie smiled at her again "My wife worked - or used to work - as a recording specialist. D'ya know that studio up in Fairbanks? She was a tech there. Gave it up a few years back though."

At this point, Harmann noticed something odd about Charlie. He seemed to bite down on his words, closing his teeth with an audible click. A narrowing of the tiny muscles around his eyes followed as Harmann watched like a predator sensing prey. What did it mean? What was Charlie hiding? He stowed the information for later. Such details required finesse and time and pressing the situation would gain him nothing.

"So, what - your wife wired you?"

Charlie shook his head "No. Dunn searched me for wires every time we met. No, she put bugs in my car, in our house, in my gun store."

Harmann frowned "But he must've spoken to you in other places."

"Sure. We got a couple of those conversations from using my cell phone but some of that is missing. Couldn't get everything."

"So, your wife is the real hero here?" Harmann couldn't resist the jibe, but Charlie didn't respond, affixing that cold glare instead.

"My client is willing to co-operate in the case against Mr Dunn." the lawyer leaned forward, all business now "I think we can help you to put Mr Dunn away for life."

"I can already do that."

"This will put the nails in the coffin, so to speak, Detective. Isn't this something we all want? William Dunn is an evil man and with my client's testimony, he will be dead and buried. Perhaps literally."

Harmann was seething with suppressed rage. Moore was

pissing him off too - why hadn't she said anything? These assholes were walking all over them and she was doing nothing. Goddamn bitch.

"What about all the money you stole?"

Charlie shrugged "What money?"

"You stole twenty million in bearer bonds as well as -" Harmann checked the paper before him "Two million from those cash machines. Where is it?"

"I don't have it. Dunn has all the details."

"Your accountant friend might know."

"He doesn't. Dunn kept all the details. Mo might know the amounts but that's hardly inside knowledge."

"So, Mo is innocent too?"

"No." Charlie shook his head "Mo was pulled in by Dunn too. I personally saw Dunn hold a gun to Mo's head on more than one occasion. He'll tell you what he can, but Dunn is your guy."

Harmann was silent. The lawyer had turned to his briefcase, busy shuffling papers. Harmann wondered if he was hiding a self-satisfied grin behind the expensive leather. Abruptly, he stood up, ordering Moore to do the same. He turned to leave, holding the door open for the redheaded Detective. As he stepped out into the corridor, he pulled the door almost closed before pausing and stepping one foot back into the room as though something had just occurred to him.

"Hey - Brooke. You know one thing you're guilty of? Being a shitty damn husband. Still, at least your missus is available now. How d'you reckon she'd feel 'bout gettin' some payback? Maybe banging the cop who puts you away would feel pretty good."

He slammed the door, a savage grin on his face.

CHAPTER 26

"Fucking asshole!" Harmann punched the wall of the corridor, startling a pair of agents who were carrying mugs of coffee down the hall.

"Everything alright, Harm?" one of them asked, concern on his face.

"All good, John."

"Alright then." with a worried look at Moore, John left.

Harmann put both hands over his face and groaned.

"Hey! It's not all bad. Charlie is gonna do some serious time here!"

Harmann surveyed her with a withering look that would've scored paint from a wall "No, don't you see what's going on here? He's gonna skate with some goddamn plea bargain here. You know he never had a firearm at all? Judge's love that. He manages to pull these recordings together, God knows what he's gonna get."

Moore blew air out of her cheeks "Damn."

Harmann turned decisively back towards the room where Mohsin sat alone "It's not over yet. We can at least get the money back this bastard stole. C'mon. Let's make this skinny little bitch sweat a little."

CHAPTER 27

Mohsin was shivering in the AC. He looked terrified as Harmann strode in, jacket tails swinging behind him. Moore stood in the doorway as Harmann began to pace up and down.

"You say Dunn had everything?"

"Yes."

"All the account numbers? All the transactions?"

A small hesitation "Yes."

Harmann whirled around, a shark smelling blood in the water "What? What did he leave you?"

Mo looked hopefully at Moore, but she was concentrating on shutting the door which had gotten stuck open.

"Over here, motherfucker! Look at me, not the lady!" to make his point, Harmann stepped around the table, slamming his palm onto the surface and leaning over Singh.

"He - he told me the account numbers once. One of the accounts."

"What for?"

"It was for the bearer bonds! He managed to get them into an account -"

"How? How'd he do that so fast?" Harmann sprayed spittle onto the man's face as he shouted. Moore had finally shut the door and was examining the lock in confusion.

"I don't know! I didn't ask-"

"Bullshit!"

"I'm not lying!"

"I know one of the accounts - it had a lot in it, five million dollars! He wired it through a couple of companies-"

"He set up shell companies?"

"Shells? No, they were legitimate. He made big orders with them and the money went through."

"Where? Where were the companies?"

"The Caribbean. All over. He spread it out."

"You better start telling us about them!" a rattling sound from the door and he shot a look at Moore "Goddamn, Detective! Can you fix that damn door, please?"

She nodded and stepped out, pulling the door closed behind her. The handle twisted a few times, then rattled. Harmann swore in frustration as he realised Moore had locked herself out. Ignoring her, he turned back to Singh, that same flash of recognition returning "I know you, don't I? I've met you before somewhere."

"I don't know-"

"What'd I bust you for? Drugs? Booze? Fraud?"

"I've never -"

"You better start comin' up with something, boy, or I might just find somethin' that I can stick to you!"

"I can tell you! I'll tell you all about them. It will take years though."

"Huh?" Harmann looked away from the door which Moore was now rattling from the outside "What are you talking about?"

"The way the system is set up. We used an algorithm. It randomly spread the accounts and breaks down the patterns."

Moore was hammering on the door "Call the damn caretaker! Stop rattling that freakin' handle!" roared Harmann but Moore didn't hear him.

"It'll take years to crack it. It's the way it's set up."

Harmann wasn't aware of grabbing Mohsin's lapel, but his hands had moved and he now towered over the younger man who stared up at him in horror, now babbling like a mad thing.

"Dunn said it was my payment - sorta thing! He said I'd only get three to five for money laundering and it'd take that long for the cops to crack the accounts and then he'd leave me some cash in there and -"

Harmann punch the man across the face. He hadn't really

meant to and if Moore had been in the room, he'd never have dared. But all he saw as he closed his eyes was that cold stare on Charlie's face and the furious realisation that the bastard was only going to get a handful of years. His temper broke and he raised his fist again, landing it with a meaty thud on Mohsin's jaw, making the young man grunt in pain.

"You can't fuckin' do that man! Fuck off me!"

Wham!

Harmann was into a stride now and he landed blow after blow a red mist settling over his vision as this squirming little weakling cringed and cried.

Smack

Smack

Smack

He pummelled the man, muttering filthy curses at Dunn, at Charlie and at Mohsin under his breath until the accountant was shaking and bruised. Blood trickled from the corner of his mouth and he was crying.

Harmann suddenly froze, the anger leaving him in a heartbeat and stared at the man "Jesus. What was I thinking?"

Damage control flashed through his mind and he tugged his handkerchief from his pocket, dabbing the blood from Mohsin's face, causing the skinny man to shriek and pull away but at that moment, the door crashed open and Moore staggered into the room, evidently having just put her shoulder to the door.

Behind her, staring open mouthed at Harmann and the bloody faced man was Finnick.

And behind him was the lawyer who was representing Charlie.

This time, it was the lawyer who narrowed his eyes and smiled like a predator. Harmann swore, looking down at Mohsin.

"Well, ain't you the luckiest thang on earth." he drawled, ignoring the terror in the man's eyes "Looks like I just got you a ticket outta here."

CHAPTER 28

"Five years."

"You're goddamn kidding me."

"You watch your damn mouth, Harmann!" Finnick's tone brooked no response other than a hastily muttered apology.

They were back in the control room. The lawyer had chased them out of Singh's room and Harmann now glared at the monitor where an agency medic was dabbing alcohol rub on the accountant's face.

"Son of a bitch is milking it!"

Finnick rounded on Harmann, melting the Detective's brash attitude "You assaulted a damn prisoner, Harm! That ain't how this agency works! We're gonna have to let him go now, you know that? He's gonna walk! I don't know what you were thinking! And you!" this last to Moore who widened her eyes in surprise "Where the hell were you? You're supposed to keep a check on your partner!"

"The door lock was busted, Sir-"

"Shut up! Shut the hell up, both of you!" Finnick stopped for a moment and closed his eyes, breathing hard through gritted teeth "Now - those recordings sound genuine and the lawyer has all but written Brooke's plea bargain out. He's gonna do about five years but I'll try and speak to the judge. It's lucky -" he loaded the words with threat "- Dunn is where he is because if he wasn't going down for attempt murder, I'd have your damn badge!" he roared the words at Harmann who lowered his eyes, hiding his fury.

"You ever make a fuckup like this again, Harm, I'll have it. Got me?"

"Yes, Sir."

"That lawyer is gonna get Mr Singh out of here in the next five minutes, mark my words and I'm gonna let him! Can you imagine if this gets into the papers?"

Harmann, wisely, said nothing.

Finnick sighed again, looking his age "Look, this is it. Apart from this -" he indicated Singh's interrogation room on the monitor "- you've both done well. This is case closed, apart from the money which we're handing over to the fiscal team. Ain't our problem. We should have court dates soon and I want you both there. Until then, I don't want to see you for a long damn time. You keep your damn noses clean and you do your jobs to the letter! Do I make myself clear, Detective's?"

"Yes, Sir."

"Yes, Sir."

"Good."

Harmann held the door open for Moore as they left the control room and followed her along the cold corridor past the interrogation rooms. They said nothing as they approached the elevator, walking in and waiting as the doors closed and the floor lurched.

"D'ya wanna go get a bite to eat?"

Moore turned to him, face on and stared at him for a one, two count before she cut him down "Fuck off, Harmann. You stay the hell away from me, got it?"

Harmann stared at her in open mouthed shock as the elevator binged and the doors opened. He was still staring in shock as she turned and walked away, her pantsuit tight over her ass. He leaned sideways to catch a final glimpse of it as the doors slid shut and then she was gone.

It was only then that Harmann realised he should've got out in the lobby with her. Now the elevator was going up and he cursed, futilely pressing the button.

Bing

He was on the same floor as his office and he sighed in annoyance before shrugging, stepping out of the elevator and striding along the hallways to his small kingdom where he locked the door, sat down behind the desk and pulled out a bottle of bourbon and a single glass.

"Here's to you, William C. Dunn." he raised the glass in mock salute to the empty room, sipping the amber liquid. Unbidden, an image of Charlie and his terrible glare rose in his mind and he took another swig, feeling the burn on his tongue.

"And fuck you too, you sanctimonious prick."

Harmann knocked back the glass and smiled to himself.

Victory was sweet - not as sweet as Moore and her tight pant suit, but sweet nonetheless. Besides, he had the bourbon and at least the bottle couldn't talk back to him. He put his feet up and turned to stare out the window to enjoy his drink.

CHAPTER 29

"These images are coming to you live from the state courthouse where Channel Nine newsreader Dianne Solihul has the latest on the trial that some are calling the case of the decade! Dianne?"

"That's right, Joe! Here on the ground the jury has just announced a unanimous guilty verdict and in a surprise twist, they have called for the death sentence for the now convicted bank robber, murderer and all round bad guy, William C. Dunn! As we know this latest in the series of trials for Dunn's spree of crimes is a conviction for the attempted murder of SATA Detective Harmann with whom Mr Dunn apparently had some kind of personal vendetta. Over a series of months following a now famous interview, Mr Dunn attempted to coerce a group of accomplices into recreating some of the most famous cases that Detective Harmann has solved over a long and illustrious career. Detective Harmann last night told reporters that he fully expected a guilty verdict and that this would be the final part in a long awaited justice process."

"And Dianne, I believe that Deputy Director Finnick of the SATA has given you some of his time?"

"That's right, Joe. Deputy Director, can you comment on what this case has meant to you and your department?"

"Well Mr Dunn is a real nasty piece of work and I have to say that this is a true victory to have a man like him off the streets. For Detective Harmann, I can confirm that this is the end in a very personal case that has taken every ounce of his professionalism and skill to bring to a safe conclusion."

"And Deputy Director, what about last month's case of Charles

Brooke, the man who was convicted of hijacking an aircraft over the state? Do you think that was a miscarriage of justice?"

"Well, in this state we rely on our judiciary system to ensure a fair trial for everyone accused of a crime and in this case, they chose to give him a sentence of five years. I believe that SATA and in particular Detective's Harmann and Moore did everything in their power to get a conviction for Mr Brooke and so I believe that this is a victory for the agency."

"But isn't it true, Deputy Director, that a third man was able to walk free without a conviction, due to negligence in the SATA investigation?"

"No, Dianne that's completely untrue. The other parties who were initially arrested in connection with these cases were released without charge because there was no evidence against them. I stand by my Detectives with complete confidence that this was indeed the case and that no-one else was involved in these terrible crimes."

"But Deputy Director, surely you can understand when the public complains that this sentence was too light? The man stole a jet plane and we all know how that has turned out in America before!"

"As always, I'll bow my head to the knowledge and fairness of the judicial system and reiterate that SATA did everything humanly possible to bring these people to justice. If people are unhappy with the decision, well they can rest assured that today a truly evil man was sentenced to death and will soon be gone from this world."

"Thank you, Deputy Director. Joe, scenes down here in the courthouse are truly chaotic as people cheer and decry the sentence but I'm sure we'll learn more about the man sentenced to die as his appeals process runs on. Back to you, Joe."

CHAPTER 30

"Sorry, mate. Do you mind swapping? Me and the missus seem to have got our numbers mixed up!"

Harmann looked up into the stereotypical face of a Londoner. Crooked teeth, bulging neck fat and a grubby polo shirt belted over blue jeans. If the man had been sporting a soccer shirt and singing God Save the Queen, he couldn't have fit more of a profile.

Harmann smiled and nodded. He stood up from the small seat which immediately sprang back into the upright position and then crammed his thighs into the cushion as the man's wife passed by. She was at least twenty years younger than the polo shirt sporting man, dressed to the nines in a black cocktail dress and heels, a glass of prosecco clutched in her heavily manicured hand. She shot Harmann a grateful smile as she passed before doing a double take as Harmann shot her a wink and a more-than-friendly grin.

"Wonderful." he murmured as she passed and eased herself into the seat he'd just vacated. He sat down, clutching his own glass of scotch and twirling the ice cubes as he leaned backwards, pretending to watch the empty stage all the while peering into the woman's cleavage.

The dull roar of hundreds of patrons settled and then died out as the lights in the theatre dropped and the great curtain on the stage swung upwards on invisible cords. Down in the stalls, Harmann had an excellent view and he grinned and applauded gently for the next hour as the actors trotted out their performances on the stage. The lights came up and people began to head for the bar or the lavatory. The polo shirt sporting man handed his companion a strip of plastic which she rewarded with a wet smooch before she turned to Harmann and prettily asked if he wouldn't mind letting her through.

"Actually, I was just headed to the bar myself." he flashed her a winning grin, offering his empty scotch as proof. The husband caught his voice and shot him a beaming grin.

"Keep an eye on 'er for me, would you, pal?" he roared with laughter for some reason.

Oh, I'll keep more than that, pal. Thought Harmann as he led the woman to the end of the row.

"I'm Harmann." he offered, holding out an unnecessary hand to help her from the row of seats.

"You're American?" she had a coarse accent, leaning too heavily on the vowels.

"Sure. On Vacation." Harmann knew from the previous weeks philandering that the British women loved to hear American words and so he kept his sentences short, heightening the sense of mystery and leaning on the vernacular, piquing their interest.

Taking no chances, Harmann offered his arm for her to hold which she took, graciously. As they approached the bar, Harmann looked askance at the queue which was certainly not his idea of a flirtatious conversation starter and so he bypassed it, ignoring the stern looks and muted anger of the British.

"What'll you have, ma'am?" he propped an elbow on the bar, heedless of the well suited businessman behind him who conceded the bar space almost automatically.

She would have a gin and tonic and Harmann waved a couple of notes at the nearest bar girl, a pretty blonde with Slavic features who smiled and served him first. He'd come to recognise that in London, Slavic features meant Slavic born and he wasted no time trying to decipher her heavy accent, turning away without the change.

"Whew. Shall we step outta the crowd?" without waiting for an answer, Harmann steered the other man's wife across the bar, taking the chance to 'accidentally' place his hand slightly lower than south.

They reached the edge of the now crowded bar to find a uniformed usher standing guard over a roped off section of corridor.

"What's down there, young man?"

The young man started at being addressed "Er - that's the private bar, Sir. It's closed tonight..." his eyes widened at the tip Harmann was handing him and a moment later, the tall American was leading the woman into the bar and the usher tried to resist the urge to stare after them.

Back in the theatre, polo shirt was staring at soccer scores on his phone, oblivious to his wife's absence. As the lights began to dim once again for the second act, she slipped back into her seat and he leaned around her to grin at the American who beamed back at him.

"Alright, love?"

"Yeah. Queue at the bar."

"Big one?"

"Oh yeah."

Harmann resisted the urge to laugh out loud as she reached a hand over, squeezing him in the darkness. Vacation wasn't so bad, he reflected.

The show ended and Harmann made himself scarce before angry husbands could seek their revenge and stepped out into the humid air. He doffed his jacket, swinging it over his shoulder and began to stroll up the sidewalk - or pavement as they called them here. The walkway was narrower than back home, something that had bothered him for a couple of days until he'd embraced the opportunity to pass close by the women who seemed to be in a constant competition to wear the least amount of clothing humanly possible the second the sun showed its face.

It could be worse.

A giant red bus roared past and he considered jumping on it and heading back to his hotel, only ten minutes from the west end but at the end of the road, a corner bar stood with its door open and a group of well-dressed young ladies had just been ushered in by the doorman and so Harmann followed them, stepping into a dark bar, smelling of wine and the strong ale they brewed here.

He'd already sat at the bar and ordered a drink - scotch, not that ale muck - when he spotted the group of girls, all plainly sprawled across the laps of a group of younger men, all with excellent tailoring. Harmann shrugged to himself, conceding defeat as he sipped at the good scotch.

"Would you like to see a bar menu?" the barman was young, thin and unsmiling. This was the custom, Harmann was realising in a culture which seemed to regard tips as a wild foreign curiosity to be marvelled at. He nodded and just as the last of the scotch vanished down his throat he watched expectantly as a surly faced teenager carried out something called a 'scotch egg' and dropped it on the bar without a word. Signalling for another drink, he bit into it and chewed thoughtfully before deciding that scotch in this case was different to the golden liquid he was drinking. Still, when in Rome.

Harmann finished as the barman poured him another. He tapped his credit card against the proffered machine, wondering why they didn't allow you to set up a tab and pay at the end. Weird. He turned on the bar stool to lean gently back against the wall which looked from the ornate wallpaper as though it should be in a museum, not a watering hole and sipped his drink slowly, watching the patrons move through the pub.

He was another two scotch's deep before the pub began to empty out. The barman began wiping the tables down and Harmann, taking his cue began to stand and scoop up his jacket. He nodded to the doorman on the way out and took a couple of steps in the night air before deciding he wasn't ready to head home. He asked the doorman who pointed him a few streets away to a whisky bar which, Harmann reflected, would probably have been his first choice. Still.

An hour and a half later and he was truly drunk. A second scotch egg had been put before him as he sat in the dimly lit bar but it had done little to soak up the strong liquor. Still, he'd explained his taste to the matronly woman behind the bar and she'd brought a succession of fine tasting drinks, each better than the last. He'd given her a good look over but even in this state he was not naïve enough to ask a woman who ran a bar to come home with him and he peaceably accepted an empty bed was no awful thing for one night.

It was then, just after midnight as Harmann was thinking pleasantly sleepy thoughts in the ancient city that unbidden, an image of Mavis Delaney, covered in the blood that had spelled her death, sprang into his mind.

Harmann lurched backwards from his table, spilling a finger of his drink and sat up, more startled than he'd ever been in his life.

"All right, love?" the barwoman had come over.

"Yes, yes. I'd like to pay." he announced, abruptly.

"'Course." she popped a check down on the table, just like back home and he added cash, struggling with the foreign notes and coins.

Bidding the bar in general goodnight which earned him more than a few curious looks, Harmann flagged down an overpriced black cab and staggered into his hotel, nodding to the night staff and leaning heavily against the mirror in the elevator.

Why had her face sprung to mind? And why now, months and months after her death? The elevator arrived at his floor and Harmann stumbled down the corridor, fishing his key card from his pocket and pressing it into the lock.

He lay on the bed fully dressed with his hands over his face as the image of her elegantly arranged golden curls matted with blood and those stupid glasses, lying half on, half off her face.

"Bitch should've ducked!" he snarled, scrambling into a sitting position. He tossed his shoes to the floor, wrenched off his necktie and hurled the jacket at the small chair by the window. The bedside cabinet concealed a bottle of shop bought scotch and he twisted the cap off, tipping it to his lips and gasping at the burning sensation.

"It wasn't fucking me." he snarled.

He drank more, forcing the liquid down until the room began to swirl and the image of Mavis Delaney blurred in his mind.

"Fucking bitch."

His stomach lurched and next thing he knew, Harmann was lurching for the en-suite, leaning over the bowl and heaving what felt like an entire bottle of good whisky into the white porcelain.

"Goddamn." he gasped, staggering to the sink. He peeled his shirt off, trying to toss it behind him but missing and dropping it in the shower instead. Another spasm heaved and he gripped the basin in both hands, the feel of the cold marble wonderful against his sweating palms. He ran the tap, watching the basin fill.

Charlie Brooke's face appeared in the swirling water, laughing and mocking him. He yelled out and slapped the water, splashing it all over the mirror. He looked up, seeing his reflection with bloodshot eyes and water dripping from his chin and the image changed to Mavis, blood dripping off her chin as her dead eyes accused him.

"Fuck you!" he screamed, trying to punch the mirror. His hand rebounded, doing no damage to the glass but he felt a dull numbness spread through the hand and stared at it in confusion.

"Bitch!" he snarled into the mirror but now it was Charlie Brooke's face, laughing at him.

"I got you! I got you, motherfucker!" he snarled and spat "I fucking got you."

Harmann sagged down onto his knees, hands still clutching the basin. He rested his forehead against the cool marble and felt his eyes droop.

"I got you. Motherfucker. I got..."

Hours later, he woke up shivering on the floor and crawled to the bed to toss and turn fitfully as laughing Charlie's and dead Mavis's chased him down long hotel corridors and into dark caves stinking of whisky.

CHAPTER 31

It was only the next morning as he bullied the restaurant staff into bringing him bacon and coffee that Harmann reflected he had no-one to talk to.

His parents were dead, his brother was an asshole somewhere in the military and his nephew was twelve. There was Finnick, but he was a boss not a friend and there was Moore, but she had made it clear she hated his guts. Various former partners sprang to mind as he mentally tallied through the people he knew.

No-one.

Maybe he needed a therapist. Dim memories of Mavis and Charlie mocking him last night floated uncomfortably close. He shook his head, looking out the window at one of London's rare heatwaves.

Harmann took a shower after kicking his only good shirt out onto the floor and left the hotel searching for one of the famous green parks in the city. He reasoned he just needed to clear his head and get thinking about something productive. It was because he'd been on vacation too long, too far out of the loop. He needed the constant pressure of a case to keep him tight and snappy, but Finnick had been right when he told Harmann to take this vacation. The long months of the trials, giving evidence and the general hauling over the coals he'd got when the Director found out he'd kicked the crap out of that accountant. No, he'd needed the break, needed to get the headspace to regain his perspective.

Now, though, he wondered if a week and a half of theatres, museums and women had been a step too far. He was, after all, a Detective by nature and without something to do, he was useless. He needed something to distract him. A bookstore beckoned conveniently and he ducked inside, addressing the proprietor who seemed unwilling to step out from behind her wooden counter but eventually she showed him the crime section and he picked up a thick novel along with a notepad and pen.

Following the woman's directions, he found himself in a wide park which several signs assured him was of great historical significance which he cheerfully ignored, instead choosing a wide patch of short grass and settling down.

As he read through the novel, he began to jot down the clues and details, building an image of the case and the characters, playing at solving the case.

By the fourth chapter, he'd decided it was the wife and he flipped to the end to discover he was right and the woman had murdered her husband in the kitchen with a frozen leg of lamb.

"Huh."

The thought flashed through his mind and then it was gone. Something to do with the novel? Harmann stared at the ornate cover with its bold lettering as a small dog came sniffing around harmlessly, a gaggle of small children not far behind as a helicopter parent hovered behind them.

"Sid! Sid!" called the small voices and the dog bounded over to them happily to receive pets and pats. Harmann stared at the dog as the parent began to eyeball him, wondering who this loner was staring at her kids.

Abruptly, Harmann looked down and whipped out his cell, dialling a plus one number and ignoring the fact that this would cost him an arm and a leg. The British dial tone jarred his ear, so much harsher than the soft American sound and he tapped his fingers impatiently on the cover of the book.

"Hello?" the voice sounded groggy, but Harmann ignored it.

"It's me. What happened to the kids?"

"Huh? Is that you, Harmann?"

"Yeah, it's me, Moore. What happened to the Brooke kids? In the case?"

"Um... I don't remember."

"Where were they when we went to the house?"

"Jesus, I don't know! What do you want from me?"

"Fuck!" Harmann shouted, forcing the kids into a stunned silence. The parent, having had enough shepherded them away from the cursive American, throwing filthy looks back over her shoulder.

"Harmann, I can't be dealing with your shit right now." Moore sounded pissed "I'm hanging up." the tone went dead.

"Fuck!" he shouted again, standing and pacing up and down, the novel forgotten on the grass. What was it? Thoughts flashed through his head in a crazed mess, logic never quite joining together. Briefly, he considered swearing again but there seemed little point. Harmann stood with his hands on his hips, staring after the small family. What did it matter? The Brooke's had children, he'd seen a photo with them. A girl and a boy. So, where'd they been when they arrived at the house? Of course, they could've been out at a friend's, out playing or any other of a thousand excuses but Harmann knew better. Something was up.

A moment later he made another call, this one to the travel department at the agency who protested that he was on vacation, that he would have to pay for the flight himself but he swore, threatened and then pleaded and thirty minutes later, checked out of his hotel and paid a small fortune for a cab to Heathrow airport.

He wrote it all down on the notepad in the departures lounge, start to finish, the entire case involving Charlie Brooke and finished with the trial just a few months prior in which the slippery bastard had got five short years for hijacking a goddamn airplane in American skies.

But that was it. He looked at the notepad, reading and re-reading the notes but it was all there. He drew a line under the sentence and a moment later, a second line beneath the first. What did it mean?

He was none the wiser an hour later when the jet left the runway and climbed, the pilot moving in a slow, wide turn as

Harmann roared back towards home.

CHAPTER 32

"So where were the damn kids?"

Anyone else - any other person in the agency would've already been shown the door to Deputy Director Finnick's luxurious office. But Harmann wasn't just anyone, he was the senior investigator and in Finnick's private opinion, the best damn cop the state or perhaps the country had ever seen. The fact that the man was a grade-A asshole only served to fuel his skill and personality as an investigator. But now, even Finnick was struggling to follow the Detective's logic.

"I don't know, Harm. At her parents?"

"Her mom's dead. Cancer. Dad was never around. No family in the immediate area either. They moved there because of the name."

"Ranger?"

"Yeah. Guess Brooke thought it'd be funny."

"But they'd been there a few years, they musta made some friends. She used to work, too. The kids were with friends that day."

A polite knock at the door and Moore walked in, her eyes narrowing at Harmann's dishevelled hair and red eyes.

"Jesus, have you slept?"

"What? No. Of course not. Here..." Harmann outlined his theory to Moore who stood with a stoic expression, bordering on disbelief.

"So?"

It was exactly what Finnick had said when Harmann had burst into his office, fresh from the airport and flushed with energy. However, Moore did not get the same restrained courtesy that the Deputy Director had got.

"So? So! Is that all you have to say? You're a goddamn Detective, Moore, or had you forgotten that?"

"Enough!" Finnick snapped and Moore bit back on the angry retort she'd loaded "Let's all remember what side we're on here. Moore - I know you two have had your differences but Detective Harmann is a damn good investigator and when he gets a hunch, it's worth listening to. Now, go over it again, slowly this time and if you don't see anything then we'll go speak to Mrs Brooke."

"No." Harmann shook his head "If there is something, we don't have enough to take any action. The case is closed, dammit and we could spook her if she really is involved somehow."

"Go on, Detective." encouraged Finnick and Harmann went over the notes he'd scribbled with Moore adding details here and there until the case was laid out before them.

"So, here's what I don't get." Moore had taken off her blazer and was sitting reversed on a chair "This guy Dunn, you've been after him for a while now?"

"Since he blasted Jerry Kaminski off the face of the earth eight years ago!"

"Right - but this guy was always the hired muscle in any team, right? The backup for the clever guys in case we ever showed up and they had to shoot their way out."

"Yeah." Harmann nodded as Finnick's eyes flicked between the two of them "But he was an opportunist, always took advantage of others if he could. Like if they gave him too many details of the plan he'd just go ahead and do it on his own. That's where he musta got the idea for the airplane job. No way he came up with that by himself."

"So, he never planned a job like this by himself?"

"I mean…" Harmann hesitated, then he closed his eyes for a long pause "Shit."

"Exactly." her ire forgotten for a moment, Moore leaned forward excitedly.

"What?" Finnick had missed a step.

Harmann turned to their boss "What she's saying, Sir, is Dunn was a muscle man. Tough guy. But this time, he stepped up to management. Now that happens, but not like this. Dunn isn't a fool, but he's a sociopath. He doesn't work with others, he stands there and looks tough while they do all the work. In fact, the reason he's been on the run so long is because he's taken out his crew on multiple occasions. That's one of the reasons he has so many identities."

"What, he took out the guys he was robbing the place with?"

"Sure. There was one, oh, fifteen years back now? Small town Pennsylvania a buncha morons outta nowheresville were knocking over seven eleven's and moved up to money trucks and banks. They hired Dunn for three or four runs and then when he'd had enough, blasted them all with the shotgun they'd paid for and walked outta the bank cool as anything."

"Damn."

"Yeah. Local cops took the view that he was some kinda vigilante who'd waited for the right moment to strike. He didn't even take the cash, left it all behind. Anyway, the point is he doesn't play well with others and he's certainly never been the brains of the outfit."

Moore frowned "I can remember a few cases in the academy where bad guys worked up from muscle to top level."

Harmann was already nodding "Sure, but they're guys who planned it all along. They work their asses off the whole way and keep doin' it once we catch 'em. Always tryna get out, tryna play the new angle but Dunn isn't like that. He's a thug."

Silence fell for a moment as the three of them cast their minds back over the long months of Dunn's trial, trying to remember the convoluted arguments as the defense and prosecution edged ever closer to an agreement.

"So, who was in charge?" Finnick played devil's advocate, letting his Detectives work it out.

Harmann said "Brooke" Moore said "Singh" and they looked at each other in surprise.

"Why Singh?" Finnick pressed.

Moore blinked for a moment before responding "Um. He's

educated, got a college degree, worked as an accountant and he was good - real good. They've recovered what, ten percent of the money?"

"Eight." Harmann grated.

"Right. So, he's a smart guy."

"No." Harmann shook his head, ignoring the flash of annoyance from Moore. He held up a peaceable hand "I get it, he's smart but there's smart and there's smart. We saw him in the interviews -" he shot a guilty look at Finnick who gestured for him to continue with a stony face "Uh - he was book smart. Guy had no street smart. No way he'd even try and approach a guy like Dunn. In fact, didn't Brooke say Dunn put a gun to the guy's head?"

"Uh-huh." Moore was nodding as the logic clicked in her mind "But Brooke..."

"Army Ranger. He'd been in combat too. Had him a couple'a medals, successful business -"

"The gun store was going under." Finnick objected.

"Sure, but only until recently. Wife said he'd started drinking - said he'd been on the wagon for a few years now, but he'd got friendly with a local barman and was drunk as hell from dawn 'til dusk. Barely opened the store."

"He wasn't like Dunn, though." Moore was speaking slowly, trying to think it through "He wasn't a sociopath. They don't let guys like that in the military, they don't play nicely with others."

"No. But he was tough enough that Dunn wouldn't scare him. And we've seen he was smart - book smart and street smart."

Finnick blew out a long exhalation and gripped the arms of his plush leather chair "I don't know, Harm. That's a damn stretch of logic and the guys are locked up now anyway."

Moore nodded her agreement.

"Five years..." Harmann shook his head as the same contemplative silence fell over the office once again.

"Okay." all eyes turned to Harmann "Okay, maybe it is a stretch, but we've all heard of worse. Say for the hell of it, Charlie Brooke is the ringleader and he - oh I don't know, coerced Dunn into thinking he was in charge. I don't know 'bout that but say he did that." he glanced at the two of them.

"Go on." Finnick encouraged.

"So, when he 'jacks that plane, he knows his face is plastered everywhere. Cameras at the airport, cabin footage on the airplane itself and then all the eyewitnesses - including a cop." he pointed at Moore.

"His face wasn't on record, though. He knew the images wouldn't get a match on any database."

"Right. But from then on, he had to go into hiding. Twenty million dollars was a lot of cash but still, new identities are expensive. He'd have had to flee the country, leave his wife and kids."

"But he didn't. He went to the bar." pointed out Moore.

"Exactly." Harmann snapped his fingers "So what if this guy knew he was gonna get caught?"

Silence fell once again but this time it was heavy with tension. The color slowly drained from Finnick's face as he leaned forward, elbows resting on the desk before him.

"The fiscal crime team - they thought it would take how long to get through that algorithm?"

"Um... With current computer technology it was designed to be broken after five years."

"And Brooke is where...?"

Moore answered that one "Asked to be locked up locally. He's in Boran minimum security."

"Five years..." Finnick's eyes had gone glazed "He could be out in what, three or four with good behaviour?"

"Yeah, but they don't usually let..." now Harmann's vision had glazed.

Finnick waited while the Detective figured it out. Moore tapped her fingers impatiently.

"Why's he want to be close to home?"

"Wife and kids..." Moore realised the error even as she said it.

"But his wife filed for divorce. He cheated on her."

"The kids then?" she suggested.

"The kids. The kids, the kids, the kids." Harmann was nodding in time with his racing thoughts "He doesn't want to be near them so he can see them. He wants to be there so when he breaks out, he can grab them and get the hell outta the country. It's easy. Minimum security, he could be on daily work details for all we know!"

"I don't think -" Moore began but Harmann had already pulled out his cell, searching for the prison phone number. He dialled and stood impatiently as Moore and Finnick exchanged frowns.

"Hello? Detective Harmann, SATA. Yes, that one. Listen - I need you to check on a prisoner for me, we have reason to suspect that Charlie Brooke may be attempting to break out of custody -" the voice cut him off and Harmann frowned, listening for a moment "No. He's what? Okay. Damn. Yes, I'll talk to the warden." hold music played.

"John Faslane is the warden." muttered Finnick "I know him - hey, put it on speaker, will ya?"

Harmann complied, laying the cell on the desk and a moment later the deep voice of the prison warden came on "John Faslane."

"John? Finnick here, over at SATA with Detective's Harmann and Moore."

"Fin! Good to hear from you. Are those the two that are responsible for filling my cells here? Good work, Detective's."

"Thank you, warden." Harmann took over the conversation "Reason we're calling is concern about Charlie Brooke. I have reason to believe that he may attempt an escape."

"Escape?" the warden sounded disbelieving "Mr Brooke is under constant surveillance at this moment. We may be a minimum-security facility but we take no chances with our new inmates. He's escorted by two men everywhere he goes and is mostly separate from gen-pop right now."

Harmann looked exasperated and turned away as Finnick took over the call "John? Would ya do us a solid and run some checks on the man for us?"

"Matter of fact I can check everything from here, Fin." there was the sound of a computer keyboard being tapped and then the warden came back "I have eyes on the man as we speak. He's in his cell right now... Oh, he's got a visitor."

"Can you tell us who?" Harmann had come back.

"Sure, everyone is checked in. Let's see... Singh. Mohsin Singh."

"Goddamn." Harmann had gone white faced and he saw the expression reflected on Moore and Finnick. He turned, wheeling for the door as Finnick scurried out from behind the mahogany desk "John? Lock the sumbitch down, lock him down and stall Singh! We're comin' as fast as wheels can move!"

CHAPTER 33

"Come on, come on!" Harmann swore as an open topped sports car overloaded with high schoolers swerved across the lane. He leaned on the horn, flipping the kids off before stomping on the gas and leaving them in his dust.

"Take a right up here." Finnick was in the passenger seat, cell open in his left hand whilst his right clutched the handle on the ceiling, knuckles white. Moore was in the backseat holding on for dear life.

"There it is!" Harmann called in triumph as the white brick of the prison loomed at the top of a gentle rise before them. A winding road approached the gates and he cursed, braking sharply and slamming through the gears as they wove back and forth. At the gates, the guard waved them through and Harmann screeched the car into the parking lot as a tall white man in a flawless suit approached, flanked by a pair of burly looking Correctional Officers dressed in riot gear.

"Fin?" the warden shook hands with the Deputy Director who hurriedly introduced Moore and Harmann. They hurried out of the sun into the cool interior of the prison where the warden insisted they walk so as not to alarm the inmates who, Harmann noticed distractedly, were mainly well dressed, quietly going about their daily business. It was a world away from the isolated supermax most of his perps went into where every guard had a shotgun and violence was the order of the day.

Five minutes restrained hurrying and they came to D block where Charlie Brooke was held. The CO in charge of the block was waiting for them and ushered them through, leading them along the metal gantry that ran the length of the tall, narrow building until they reached an open door with the legend 'BROOKE, C' stamped on the wall in black paint.

"Brooke! On your feet, son." called the CO before stepping first into the cell "Warden's here to see ya."

The warden stepped in, followed by Finnick and then Harmann moved in. The cell was surprisingly spacious with a comfy looking bed, a console on which a widescreen TV stood and a small table with a pair of chairs. Standing by one of these chairs, clearly having only just vacated it was Charlie Brooke who stared with an expression of surprise, swiftly turning to shock as Harmann and Moore entered the cell.

A flurry of movement and Harmann saw the other chair was occupied by Mohsin Singh who cringed back at the sight of him.

"Uh - good morning, Mr Brooke." Finnick was all professional "I can see you have Mr Singh here with you."

"Deputy Director, warden, Detectives." Charlie looked wary "What's goin' on?"

"We wondered if you'd be able to tell us that." Harmann had stepped forward, getting closer to Charlie. He realised that the man was taller than him, something he'd missed in the interrogations and the trial. He had to look up at the former Ranger who blinked in surprise.

"I'm just sittin' here talkin' with my friend." he gestured at Mo who nodded.

"'Bout what? 'Bout escaping?"

"Escaping? Detective, I ain't tryna escape." Brooke cast a furtive glance at the warden who cleared his throat.

"Detective -"

"We know you masterminded this whole thing, Brooke. You faked Dunn bein' in charge, but you wanted to get caught all along. Five years? You ain't gonna be here for five years. Why don't cha tell us what the two of you are plannin'?"

"I ain't plannin' nothin'. Wanted to get caught? Sure. That way you got me outta this situation. I - we -" he gestured at Singh "- we never wanted to be caught up in this! I had a business, a life and that asshole used us to get what he wanted. No, I promise you Detective, I have no plans to escape. I'll do my time and move on with my life."

"Detective, Fin, I must protest! This man is under my custody and he has done nothing wrong. I promise you, Mr Brooke has been nothing but a model prisoner in the months he has been here with us and I see no reason why he will not be fully rehabilitated and ready to re-integrate into society! I must ask you to step back and lay off him! I see no reasonable evidence for you bein' here!"

Harmann seethed, he hadn't stepped back. He looked into those deep black eyes, seeing none of the disgust and hatred that Charlie had showed in the interrogation room. Instead, what he saw there made him more confused and pissed off than ever. Because Charlie was telling the truth.

"Goddamn." Harmann stepped back and the warden moved to stand between him and Brooke. In doing so, he revealed Singh who was still sat in the small chair, eyes flicking back and forth.

"And what are you doin' here? Helpin' to plan another robbery? Helpin' him escape?" Singh cowered before the man who had brutalised him as the warden's voice rose in protest.

A firm hand gripped Harmann by the upper arm and he turned in surprise to see Finnick's furious expression. Without a word, he marched the Detective from the cell and bade him leave the block, telling the CO to escort Harmann back to their car. Then, he turned to the warden and Harmann heard the beginning of a laborious apology but then he was being marched back along the gantry and out through the prison.

"Harmann?" Moore had come with him and she hurried to catch up "That ain't your fault, what happened back there. We all thought it was true."

"Sure." Harmann didn't know what else to say. As he stepped out the door of the block into the midday heat, he felt the anger leave him in a flash, in its place a wash of exhaustion and fatigue gripped him and he leaned against the white bricks for support.

"You okay?"

"Yeah. Just need a minute."

"Alright, I'll get you some water. There's some in the car, hang on." Moore stepped away.

Harmann closed his eyes, leaning his upper back on the bricks and rubbed his eyes. He'd been so sure, so certain but now, seeing Brooke in his cell, he knew he'd been wrong, that the hunch had been nothing more.

A car door slammed and he blinked, realising he'd rubbed too hard and his vision was now fuzzy. Moore was walking back towards him, but he frowned, certain they had parked in the other direction. Had she lost the car? Stupid bitch.

"Detective?"

He furiously fisted his eyes again, clearing the last of the haze and blinked stupidly at the sight of the woman before him.

"Goddamn." he swore, more confused than ever because the woman standing before him, a sheepish expression on her face was none other than Yvonne Brooke.

CHAPTER 34

"Mrs Brooke?" Moore had caught up and joined them in the shade. Charlie's wife turned and nodded in greeting.

"What are you doin' here?" even as he said it, Harmann knew it was a dumb question.

"I'm visitin' him." she looked faintly embarassed at the admission.

"Him? After everything he did to you?" Moore sounded furious.

"I know." Yvonne hung her head, avoiding meeting their eyes "I know he's no good but he's my husband and he's sorry and he's cleanin' his act up and we're tryna make it work."

Harmann was gobsmacked at her words. He shook his head, turning away in disgust.

"Ma'am? I wonder if you could tell us where your kids were that day we arrested your husband?"

"Huh?" Yvonne looked up, confused "Why - they were just down the street. Friend of mine had them for the day because she knew I was upset."

Harmann did not turn back to meet Moore's eyes. Instead, he screwed up his own and cursed long and loud, the sound never leaving the privacy of his mind.

"Detectives!" this next voice was Finnick and he sounded pissed. Harmann turned to see Mrs Brooke had gone inside and Finnick was now striding purposefully towards them. He braced himself but Finnick spoke evenly.

"Harm, I get it. But this time you were wrong. We were all wrong. It happens. Moore, any more details come up on this case, you're in charge. Not Harmann, you. You got that, Harm? Good.

I need you to get this outta your head so you can think clearly. This -" he gestured at the building behind them "- ain't doin' no-one no good. Got it?"

"Yes, Sir." Harmann's face was almost crestfallen.

"Look, I ain't mad! You did good, you just got it wrong." Finnick sighed "Look – Singh bein' here checks out. He's been seein' a therapist 'bout the whole thing. She told him to come talk to Charlie, said it would help to lay it all out. Warden says it's all pretty normal in here. Part of the rehabilitation process."

Harmann gave a small nod and Finnick stepped forward, clapping him on the arm "You did good, Harm but you need a break. And I don't mean goin' to shows and dippin' your dick in every woman you see down in London. Look, you a few days left of vacation and I'm givin' you another week. I got Jenson and Hopkins flyin' up to British Columbia tonight for an extradition. Warden and I have just spoken and he's sympathetic. He says he knows a guy up there who has a pretty little huntin' cabin and you're goin' there 'til I say so. Get out in the wild, Harm, get your head clear. Go nail a few deer, some bears and live wild for a bit, alright? Warden's doin' you a big favour with this and so am I. I don't want you jettin' back down here with another hunch. You get an idea? You call me and I'll make sure it gets done. You got that, Harm?"

"Yes, Sir."

"Good. Moore? Drive him back to the city. I'll get a ride from one of the CO's just as soon as I'm done smoothin' things over."

"Alright, Sir. C'mon, Harmann."

CHAPTER 35

Three years later

"Sir?"

Harmann ignored the voice, tapping away at the keyboard of his laptop, finishing the email with a flourish and watching his elaborate digital signature apply itself automatically.

"Director?"

His secretary, a middle aged square shaped woman named Kathy who daily ruined her boss's fantasies of juicy young twenty-somethings in tight skirts and heels.

"Director Harmann, it's Director Finnick..."

Goddamn

"Alright, Kathy. I'll take the call."

She vanished back into the generous atrium leading to his office and a moment later, the handset on the desk clicked and Finnick's voice emanated with a faint crackle.

"Harm? The AG is here with me."

"Ma'am." Harmann straightened unconsciously behind his desk as the clipped tones of the state Attorney General sounded.

"Harmann? How you likin' the new office?"

"Oh, very nice indeed, ma'am!" Harmann affected his best brown-nosing tone. As he'd learned eighteen months previously, pleasing the AG was the route to success and he was constantly aware that the luxurious appointment to Director of Investigations - an office that hadn't existed until his appointment - was held at her whim.

"Good. I can't tell you how much we appreciate being able to rely on a good man in your position. Director Finnick has told me how much you've helped his transition to the new role. I know he only took the extension from his retirement because he had you to rely on."

"Thank you, ma'am. That's a very thoughtful thing to say. I do appreciate that a great deal." Harmann rolled his eyes at his own ass-licking tone.

"Director Finnick and I were just talkin' here..." Harmann cringed, wondering what laborious task was soon to fall at his feet.

"See, we're tryna work on the agency's public persona as you know." Harmann flinched, hoping they wouldn't send him on another round of delivering carefully worded talks to school auditoriums, packed with bored kids. He'd argued for weeks with the PR people, spinning them tales of high-speed pursuits, gunfights, firing rifles from helicopters and heated interrogations but they'd wanted the image of the agency to be professional. Sharp suits and sunglasses, never revealing the dirty, sweaty reality of law enforcement.

"Yes, ma'am."

"So, the PR people have advised us that there just ain't enough women in senior positions in the agency. We need you to consider a couple of promotions... Some high-profile positions that will get people's attention."

"Of course, ma'am." Harmann was certain the AG would hear his eyes rolling over the phone. These damn diversity quotas were spoiling the upper echelons of the agency with morons still wet behind the ears giving ludicrous orders to twenty-year detectives who no more needed a chaperone than Harmann himself. He'd listened sympathetically to the complaints and rants from good cops, overlooked for a nice office job and tried to play the political game but if he was honest, he saw their point of view perfectly and he gritted his teeth as he waited for the bombshell.

"Now, it ain't our place to tell you how to do your job-" the AG continued. Harmann made a face. By definition it was her place to tell him exactly how to do his job. Stupid bitch.

"But, if you'll cast your mind back, oh, three years or so, you might remember workin' with Detective Moore."

"Yes, ma'am."

"What was your assessment of her as an officer?"

Ass like a porn star, attitude like a damn polar bear he thought to himself as his voice gave a measured, professional assessment.

Finnick's voice came back on the line "The AG had cause to meet Detective Moore last week and was mighty impressed by her professionalism as an officer. I wonder if you'd consider elevating her to a new position in that department - Deputy Lead Investigator?"

Deputy Lead Investigator? Harmann almost swore in frustration. He could hear the well concealed strain in Finnick's voice. If the damn agency added any more managerial positions, it was going to topple over from all the weight at the top. By Harmann's count, nearly forty percent of the damn agency was in a 'Director' or 'Lead such and such' position and he himself had been drawn, albeit unwillingly, into the bureaucratic quagmire, grinding his teeth as he did so. It was only Finnick's constant reassurance that the current political climate would shift, that the agency still had its boots firmly on the ground, that kept Harmann from threatening resignation. Instead, he took solace in the oversized office, the extra digits on his paycheck and the sweet dental package the AG had thrown in.

"Oh, that sounds like a mighty fine appointment, Sir." he wondered if the AG would hear his jaw clenching or the desk creaking as he gripped it with all his strength "I'll give Detective Moore a call right away."

"Thanks, Harm." the AG sounded pleased. That was a good thing, Harmann reminded himself.

"Would you give us a call when she's - I mean when you've spoken to her?" Finnick sounded plaintive and Harmann realised his boss was up against some unseen pressure here.

"Sure. I'll call her now." Harmann hung up and barked at Kathy to summon Detective Moore.

CHAPTER 36

"Detective."

"Director."

Harmann flicked the ghost of a smile "Jealous?"

No love had been lost between them in three years and Harmann had expected this to cool his desire for the red-haired bitch that sat opposite but instead, it made him all the more fierce for her. Every time he laid eyes on her his mind raced with frantic, hot scenes where violence and sometimes even firearms featured. All perfectly legal, of course, but with a fanatical shared hatred that exploded in red hot passion.

"What can I do for you?" her voice was as cold as ice. He wanted to scoop her up and take her right there on the desk, but the mass of solid oak formed an impassable barrier between them.

"I want to offer you the position of -" he leaned forward to check his notepad "Deputy Lead Investigator." he sat back and waited for her riposte.

"Sounds good. When do I start?"

Harmann missed a beat. She certainly hadn't and her swift response threw him off.

"Don't you want to take some time to consider it?"

She shrugged "If you're offering it to me then it ain't comin' from you. It's from Finnick or more likely - the AG."

Harmann nodded slowly "The Director said you spoke to her last week?"

"Yes."

"Care to tell me what about?"

"No."

Silence.

Harmann coughed "Anyway, the job's yours. AG is pretty generous with the package." he waved a careless hand at his opulent office.

"Sure."

Harmann exhaled a deep sigh "Damn, Moore. You drive a hard-ass line with me, don't you?" he grinned.

She did not "I drive the lines I need to, Director. Are we done here?"

He rolled his eyes but nodded and Moore abruptly stood up, smoothing the lines of her suit so the jacket hung down over her ass as she turned, missing Harmann's deep scowl.

The door opened and Kathy ducked in, smiling apologetically at Moore as she left "Sir? Mail for you. Says its urgent."

Frowning, Harmann took the preferred envelope and flicked his Wilson Rapid Response knife from his pocket, the razor-sharp blade parting the paper easily. Kathy turned and walked back to her own desk, exchanging some unheard pleasantries with Moore, who, Harmann knew, curried favour with all the female secretaries.

"Moore! Moore! Get back in here, now!" he suddenly roared, startling the two women.

"What?" she stood petulantly outside his door.

"Detective Moore! That's a goddamn order!" he roared, slamming a hand on the desk.

Dislike or not, Moore was still under his command and she hastened back inside his office, shutting the door behind her, sealing Kathy's shocked face in the lobby.

"What?"

In response, Harmann flung the letter at her. Confused, she managed a fumbling catch and stared at the brief words on the otherwise blank page.

YOU KILLED MAVIS DELANEY

"Jesus..." Moore dropped the letter on the desk, turned and hauled the door open. She barked a flurry of orders at Kathy who scooped up her phone and began dialling internal numbers.

Within seconds, suited agents had filled the office, hands on their weapons. Harmann stood by as his office became the most efficient crime scene in the agency's history. The letter and its envelope were photographed in infinite detail, scooped into an evidence bag and rushed off to Dr Gilruth's lab. Harmann and Moore were swabbed and tested for hazardous agents, Moore breathing a sigh of relief when the green LEDs flashed across the gear. Seasoned detectives stood uneasily, unable to assume their usual command in Harmann's presence. Eventually, Moore chased them all out and poured Harmann a generous few fingers of bourbon.

"Sit." she directed him to his chair.

"Ice." he muttered, indistinctly.

"Huh? Oh. Kathy?" ice retrieved, Harmann took a sip, turning it into a deep swig and finally draining the glass with a gasp.

"You wanna tell me who sent that?" Moore had leaned against the desk, arms folded.

Harmann looked up at her and blinked in confusion "How the hell should I know?"

"You're the one who got it. In my experience, people don't send cryptic notes 'less they want you to know who sent 'em."

"Goddamn."

Harmann sat for a moment, face in his hands.

"Did you kill her?"

He shook his head "No."

"Was it investigated?"

"'Course it was fucking investigated, Moore! Where do you think you are?"

"I think I'm in a place you got away with beating the crap outta a guy to get a confession."

Harmann looked up at Moore, holding her gaze for a threatening two second count "You wanna talk like that, you can get the fuck outta my office."

Moore sighed in exasperation before closing her eyes for a moment "Alright. That wasn't helpful. I'm sorry."

Harmann nodded.

"So, who sent you the damn letter?"

It was Harmann's turn to sigh in exasperation before he paused, shook his head and then considered "That reporter. Taff? Tadd. Tagg! Tagg - that was it."

"The one who did the interview?"

"Yeah. He had a guy with him, camera guy. Hipster type, beard and all the gear." Harmann absently tapped his earlobes "Casey." he looked up at Moore, steel back in his gaze "That's your guy."

"I'll go get him." Moore swept out of the office, shutting the door behind her.

Harmann sat for a moment, limp in his chair as he stared, unblinkingly at the desk before him. The opulence of the office seemed to fade as Moore left but it had nothing to do with her exit. Instead, the blood-soaked curls of an old lady seemed to float before him, as clear now as they had been three years prior. Her ridiculous glasses lay on the floor next to her dead face, still hanging on by that thin strap.

"Goddamn bitch!" he hissed, shaking his head. Harmann reached for the bottle, fumbling the cap before he managed to twist it off and threw it away, hearing it bounce into the corner. He tilted the amber liquid, staring in consternation at his hand as it trembled and the glass clinked noisily.

"Fuck you, you dumb bitch! Should've kept your head down." he poured the bourbon, slamming it back with a gasp.

He closed his eyes, rubbing his knuckles hard into the lids as Mavis Delaney's dead eyes accused him. Then, in a flash, the face changed. Now it was the deep black bottomless pits of Charlie Brooke, laughing at him.

"I got you, you motherfucker!" Harmann grated out, hands clenched into fists "I got you-"

His mouth fell open as the thoughts began to spin through his mind. He stopped, hardly daring to breathe as he waited for the idea to fully form in his head.

Click!

There!

Harmann rose to his feet, hands slapping his jacket for his

cell and he tugged it out, muttering as he scrolled through the contacts with shaking hands.

"I got you, motherfucker! I got you!" but now he wore a grin of pure joy and his voice was no longer a plea of denial but a chant of victory.

"Moore? Yeah, go to the prison, go see Charlie Brooke. It's him. He sent the damn letter! I don't care about Tagg! Fuck him! Go see Brooke. Kick his ass for me!" he hung up.

"I got you, you motherfucker!"

CHAPTER 37

"Wasn't him."

"The hell it wasn't! Ask him again!"

"What d'you want me to do, keep askin' him until he loses his mind? I asked him, he showed me the system. It's all here on the computer, Harmann. Brooke hasn't sent a single bit of mail since he got here."

"Well, he told someone else to, then!"

"Tagg?"

"Fuck Tagg!"

"Goddamnit, Harmann! Get a grip, will ya?" Moore's voice was furious down the tinny phone line. Harmann resisted the urge to throw his cell at the wall "Look, what about the mail service? It came to HQ, right? Didn't someone check what company delivered it?"

Harmann grunted in surly acknowledgement.

"Alright. Harmann? I'll go get Tagg and bring him in. But this is all done by the book. I interview him, not you. Deal?"

Harmann hung up without answering.

Then he punched another number, dialling one of the senior detectives that now worked for him.

"Mitch? Yeah, it's me. Look, you got that courier company yet? Alright. No, fine. Bring it up here when they get back, alright? I don't want this over the phone. Damn thing has me all jittery. Yeah. Alright, Mitch."

He hung up and immediately the phone began to ring. Finnick.

He swore, then breathed, then answered "Sir."

"Harm? Have you seen the news?"

"No? What happened?"

"Someone sent a letter to the news. Same one you got."

Harmann stormed out of his office, cell still pressed to his ear. Kathy looked up, startled as he snatched the remote from her desk, pointing it at the small TV that hung on the wall. He thumbed the buttons furiously, ignoring Finnick in his ear.

"... Anonymous note accusing Director of Investigations Harmann of the SATA of the unlawful killing of Mavis Delaney who died in a shootout during a bank robbery gone wrong three years ago. The note states that the author has proof of this fact and will share this with us in the near future. It should be noted that as of yet, there is no evidence to substantiate these claims.

"Fuck!" Harmann threw the remote at the TV.

"Harm! This is not the time for bad publicity! We need to show the AG that we're in control of things, dammit!" Finnick's voice was laced with panic "Get this damn letter sender locked up, you got it?"

CHAPTER 38

The control room was quiet and cool, the air conditioning bringing a slight chill to Harmann's neck as he stood over the tech who had dialled the volume up to full for the Director.

Tagg and his friend Casey had co-operated with Moore's request and come willingly to the interview rooms, something that Harmann acknowledged to himself, he could not have achieved. In fact, he'd stayed well out of sight and would remain so as Moore smiled and charmed the two men.

But Harmann was not getting any warm fuzzy feelings as he watched the two men. They both wore expressions of genuine surprise at the revelation of the anonymous letters and stated categorically that they were not behind them. Harmann distinctly saw the moment that Moore gave up, flicking a glance at the camera where she knew he was watching from. Frustration gnawed at him but there was nothing to be done. They had no right to detain these two and no proof. The letter and its envelope had contained no fingerprints nor DNA and right now, Harmann was feeling the case slipping through his fingers like dry sand.

The door opened and a florid man in a cheap brown suit barged in.

"Hey, Harm."

"Mitch." Harmann shook hands with the detective with whom he held a mutual respect. Mitch handed him a case folder and immediately began running his mouth as he turned to Moore on the screens.

"Damn, but that is one fine lookin' piece of ass! You tapped that yet, Harm? Harm?" he turned to see Harman poring over the records the courier company had provided.

"You read this?" he asked Mitch incredulously.

"Yeah. Didn't make no sense to me, neither. I had the girl double check and even got her boss on the line but he said it was all straight shootin'."

Movement on the monitors drew Harmann's attention and he saw Moore leaving the interview room, passing Tagg and Casey to a uniformed guard to be escorted from the building. A moment later, she stepped into the control room, shivering at the drop in temperature. She nodded to Mitch who beamed at her before she glanced at Harmann.

"Mail?"

"Yup. Plot thickens. Damn letter was sent three years ago."

"What?"

Harmann handed her the dossier which she snatched from him before blinking in surprise "Goddamn."

The detective in Mitch had finally stopped trying to peer down Moore's blouse and had clawed his way back to reality "That raid was what, two weeks before this?" he tapped the date on the piece of paper, headed with the courier company's branding.

Moore peered at it "Yeah. Letter was sent exactly two weeks after she was killed." she looked up at Harmann "So it could've been Brooke."

"Why would Brooke send you a letter about Mavis Delaney?" Mitch protested "Two cases had nothin' to do with each other."

"There's a connection." Harmann was adamant "It's all that black bastard's fault! Goddamn Brooke! I knew he was the ringleader in all this!"

Moore shot Mitch a worried glance and the older Detective clapped a hand on Harmann's shoulder "Now, Harm, don't you be startin' all that up again! Took me months of gettin' wasted with ya to stop you goin' on like that. Brooke is in jail, he ain't no mastermind nor nuthin' besides."

Harmann ignored his friend, starting to pace up and down the control room.

"Maybe they were related?"

"Brooke and Delaney? Wrong race, Harm." Mitch shook his head.

"Brooke is dark, Harmann." Moore pointed out "No way he's mixed race."

"Then maybe Brooke was screwing her!" Harmann rounded on the two of them "We know he was cheating on his wife. Maybe he liked old white women?"

"Didn't look like it from that video." Moore pointed out "She was a pretty young thing."

"Damn straight!" Mitch chortled "We all got a good look at that. Shame we never saw the endin'..."

"She was too old." Harmann was shaking his head at his own suggestion now "No, I don't buy it..."

"What about the wife? Yvonne?"

Mitch leered at Moore "You think she was bangin' the old lady? Damn, you got a dirty mind, Moore!"

Moore ignored the comment as Mitch guffawed "I mean what if she was the mother-in-law? Yvonne's mom?"

Harmann frowned, pausing in his pacing for a minute. He thought hard, trying to piece together thoughts from years ago. Finally, he shook his head "Nah. We went over her details, over everything. I'd have remembered it."

Moore blew air out of her cheeks in frustration "Well, better go over it again. I'll pull the records." she turned to leave but Harmann spoke.

"No. We'll all go. We'll bring 'em up to my office and get this sorted out." he led the way.

CHAPTER 39

"Goddamn fuckin' military!" snarled Harmann, banging down the phone. Before him, he, Moore and Mitch had covered his desk in the case files, poring over every detail as Harmann checked the system on his laptop.

"No dice?" Mitch looked unsurprised "If he was spec ops, they keep those records tight."

Moore shoved a piece of paper forward that they'd already seen "We got his details here. Father unknown, Mother Fonda NLN - no last name."

"We can appeal to the military." Mitch leaned forward "I got some contacts I could probably call."

Moore nodded but Harmann was shaking his head "No. That's not it." he sighed deeply, his shoulders seeming to sag as energy left him "Look, it's probably just some damn goofball thinks he can get attention by dropping cryptic notes. That raid was on TV for god's sake, a million people saw it."

"There ain't no evidence, either." Mitch sounded relieved that Harmann seemed to be dropping it "That stuff they promised to send to the news? If they had the proof, why didn't they send it? Naw, if you had dirt like that then they'd have already dumped it. You ain't the kinda guy to be played with and anyone knows that. Besides, I was part of the investigation. There was nothin' doin' about that old lady. Wrong place, wrong time."

Moore slumped back in her chair. She felt strangely defeated and she saw the expression reflected in Harmann's face "Alright." she stood up and Mitch made to leave.

"Harm? I'll make those calls to my guys in the military. Might be nothin' but if it gives you peace of mind, we can do it.

Alright?"

"Yeah. Thanks, Mitch."

To Moore's surprise, Harmann held her gaze for a second, for once the carnal desire that seemed to accompany every expression was hidden. He gave her a small, sad smile and she was astonished to feel a wave of pity rise in her.

"Moore?" Mitch was holding the door open, beaming hopefully at her.

She glanced at him, then back to Harmann who seemed to give her a small shake of the head, an indication that all was well, perhaps. Sighing, she allowed Mitch to usher her out the door, leaving Harmann alone with a look of resigned defeat on his face.

CHAPTER 40

"I'm sorry about this, Mr Brooke, I'll have it sorted out in a moment." Tagg shot the target of his interview an apologetic smile and turned back to his laptop screen.

"Probably the wi-fi in here. Warden says he's havin' it extended but we ain't seen nothin' yet." Charlie Brooke grinned at Tagg to show him he was not bitter.

"It's this new recording equipment. My camera guy, Casey hooked me up with it, but trouble is, it uploads directly to the cloud so it has to have an internet connection."

"Sounds complicated." Charlie watched as Tagg disconnected, then reconnected to the network for the tenth time "I s'pose that makes it more secure though?"

"Oh, it does for sure. But the real reason is Casey can start editing right away. That gives us a head start because news is all about being the first one with the scoop these days."

"I hope an old con like me isn't much of a scoop!" Charlie chortled.

Tagg flushed "No! I mean - it's all about having the best gear and practicing with it."

"I hear that. When I was in the military, that's all we did was train. Best way to learn somethin' is to do it." he nodded sagely at his own words.

Tagg suddenly clapped his hands in success "We're in! Alright!" he turned to Charlie who smiled expectantly.

"We good?"

"I am if you are? Good." Tagg cleared his throat and arranged his notepad on his leg, checking the angle of the camera from the digital feed his laptop screen was showing him "Mr Brooke, perhaps you could begin by introducing yourself?"

Charlie smiled "Sure. My name is Charlie Brooke, I'm currently three years into a five year sentence for robbery."

"And, if I may Mr Brooke, we're all familiar with your face now. I wonder, could you answer a few details we'd love to know about the crimes that you were accused of perpetrating-"

"Convicted. I was convicted of perpetrating. I confessed fully and take total responsibility for my actions."

"Right. Now, about three years ago I interviewed a man named Harmann who was at the time the lead investigator for the State Appropriation and Theft Agency. We discussed some of the more famous cases that he'd been responsible for solving, including the notorious TT gang robberies and the failed hijacking of Flight 72A9. Now, surely you must understand why some people say that your crime spree three years ago was based on the details revealed in this interview?"

"Of course. I've made no attempt to hide such details. You see, I was in a low point in my life. I'd dishonoured my wife, she'd lost her job and possibly her career and I'd been drinkin' more than was good for me. My gun store was failing as a result and I was lookin' for an easy way out."

"And so, you saw the interview and decided to work your own version?" Tagg pressed.

"No, not exactly." Charlie frowned to himself as he thought back "See, there was this man who called himself Will Dunn. Used to think that was a fake name - sounded too much like 'well done', ya know? Anywho, this guy showed up in Ranger 'bout a month before the first robbery we did and starts slinging his weight about in the bar I drink in. Put a friend of mine on his ass for no good reason and so Mr Dunn and I had a little conversation out back - if ya know what I mean - and I showed him how to treat people better."

"You mean you got the better of him?"

"Well..." Charlie shifted sheepishly "'Afraid not. See, I got me a good few shots in but then he pulls a gun on me. Damned if I was too drunk to pull my own piece. 'Course, Dunn weren't no good man and he doesn't leave it at that. I thought he might kill me, but it turned out it was much worse."

"How so?"

"He made me drive him to my home. Gun to my head, I didn't see no other way. When he got there, he stopped, said he knew where I lived now and that was it. Then he just up and left. Thought that was the end of it."

"Didn't you call the cops?"

"And what? Get arrested for a DUI? Local deputies weren't too pleased with my behaviour of late, either. I'd been makin' a fool outta myself drinkin' too much and they'd already warned me. Naw, I decided it was time to quit the bottle after that."

"So, when did you see Dunn again?"

"Next day. Sumbitch shows up to my house and just opens his car door, like in a movie. Goes 'Get in'. So, I did. Drives me over to this place he's layin' low in where he's got the third man, little Asian dude called Singh. Says he's the accountant and together the three of us're gonna knock off thirty million dollars."

"Thirty million! That must have seemed incredible."

"Tell the truth, I didn't believe a word of it. The guy was unstable, clearly -"

"Dunn?"

Charlie nodded "That's right, Dunn. Singh was normal enough. Scared lookin' kid, way outta his depth. Turned out Dunn had found him through a Craigslist ad for help with business tax and scared the guy into helpin'."

"Now, Mr Brooke, this is where a lot of people struggled to believe your story." Tagg gave an apologetic smile "See, you were an army Ranger, did some spec ops and black ops stuff that I can't find any unclassified documents about. If I may say so, you'd been around violence and bad guys your whole life, what stopped you ending Mr Dunn's career once and for all?"

"It's a good question, Tagg. Thing is, Dunn was good - still is although he's on death row now so he can't be that good. But Dunn was always armed, always watchin'. He never got in a car with me again unless he was in the backseat with the seat belt fastened and his gun in his hand. He was damn fine with that piece, too. Had him a Colt 1911 and a couple'a spare mags he never moved without. There was one time that Singh gave him some backchat, too, can't remember exactly what over but I remember the room freezin' and I thought he was about to knock some sense into the guy but instead he throws some weird kung-fu shit at him and gets him in one of the best chokeholds I ever seen. Quick as that -" Charlie snapped his fingers "Guy could fight and had done it before. Maybe I coulda taken him back in my prime but who knows. More likely I ended up shot and then he went after my family. No, I decided the safest course of action was to keep my eye on him and see this whole pile of shit through."

"Now, during the bank robberies, the three of you were notorious for not firing a shot. In fact, it's only Dunn who held a weapon. Why was that?"

"See, Dunn had a good plan. Gotta give credit where it's due. Those banks were all trading under different names but they were all part of the same parent company. And they had policies like most cash bein' kept in the cash machines and few staff on during the day that made them a ripe target for a man like Dunn. That's how Singh was useful. He was good with computers - I mean, he was an accountant, but he knew algorithms like... I don't know. Like somethin' that knows algorithms. I watched him write code once and it was like seein' a mad thing dance across the screen. Guy was - still is - a genius. So, when Dunn found out about these banks and their systems, the two of them realised they could break the machines open in a few seconds. In, out, no-one needs to get hurt. Besides, the companies didn't give a damn. They were insured up to their eyeballs. They didn't even bother sending someone to the trial!"

"Could you tell us more about how you opened the cash machines?" Tagg pressed, glancing at his list of notes.

"I can, but I ain't an expert and I weren't exactly in a position to ask questions." Charlie smiled "But it seems the staff in the bank each mornin, they'd take the cash outta the vault and then they had a key card they swiped on the machines and it all went in, simple as anythin'. We watched a couple of them through the glass in the mornings before they opened. Whole process took less than five minutes. And that was what Dunn wanted."

"I see." Tagg nodded "And that was the program that Singh wrote? He cloned the key cards?"

"Basically. But he didn't want to. I don't know what Dunn had on him, but the kid was terrified outta his mind."

"And the airplane heist? Was Mr Singh part of that?"

"Not the actual job, no. That was all me. See, Dunn had figured it all out, said he'd been workin' on it for years and I believe the man because damn me if it weren't all spelled out, pretty as anythin'. He'd had enough by this point and needed to get rid of me. 'Course, murderin' me was one option but he decided on a better way. He figured if I took the fall for his dirty work then he'd get away and no-one would know he was there."

"Except you."

"Right, but remember he knew where we lived, knew my wife's name, my kids' schools and that was enough for me. With me in the pen and him free out there? No, Sir! I ain't the kinda guy who'd leave my family unprotected like that. No way. If it'd come to that, I'dve kept my mouth shut forever."

"What happened on the airplane?"

Charlie shrugged "Nothin' you didn't see reported already. I had a fake ID card, but it was an internal charter flight. They ain't as strict on security and stuff. I made the bomb - although there was never any explosive in it. I knew how to make it look real from my time in the military and so I just boarded the airplane and at a certain point, I handed the hostess a note."

"You nearly got away with it, too!"

"Sure! 'Course, we knew that company had skydiving rigs aboard so that part was always easy. What was hard was foolin' the boys in the Air Force. 'Course, it weren't their fault. I always had the greatest respect for our men and women who still wear their uniforms."

"Of course." Tagg hastened to add "Now, Mr Brooke, if I may

speak candidly, you seem a pretty decent sorta guy to me."

"Well, thank you kindly!"

"I mean it! Would you say you've turned your life around?"

"Well, I'm still in jail so not quite. But yes, I think that from now on, I will live a life of peace. I'm a long way from being a good guy, Tagg, but I'll do my best to make my peace with the world."

"And to the victims of the crimes?"

"Yes." Charlie's voice became sombre "I'm real sorry to those people I scared. I did my best in every situation to lessen the fear and stress on the bystanders. I'm sure plenty of them are workin' it out in therapy still but, I know I did my best given the circumstances. For the money itself, I understand the insurance companies managed to cover it so that's a relief to me. I'm just glad that no-one got hurt durin' all this non-sense."

Tagg cleared his throat, looking at the last question on the page "And, if there were one positive, Mr Brooke, to this whole sorry ordeal...?"

Charlie looked down for a few long seconds. He fiddled with his hands and nodded slowly to himself before he raised his head, eyes locked on the small lens "I'd say it's a mighty good service to the world that William C. Dunn is gonna have his life ended by the state. That man is pure evil and I'd be mighty glad if the state would see fit to send him straight to hell."

"Thank you, Mr Brooke."

CHAPTER 41

Four weeks later

Harmann sat in the leather chair that had once been Finnick's, his mood as black as the sky outside. The storm hung in the air, humidity like a physical weight and small shocks of static sparked from every surface.

A stack of letters lay in an untidy pile on Harmann's desk. Every one contained the same cheap printed text, on a cheap white paper.

MAVIS DELANEY SENDS HER REGARDS

For the first time in thirty years, SATA had failed Harmann. No one, from forensic specialists to hot headed Detectives had been able to determine the source of the letters. One had arrived each day, some in the morning, others as Harmann wrapped up after a long day of procrastinating, picking the letters up, reading them and putting them back down.

He'd stopped being angry. He'd bypassed scared. Now, he simply sat and stared, biting the head off anyone foolish enough to disturb him.

He'd stopped drinking. It was no comfort anymore, brought no escape from the words that filled every waking moment.

MAVIS DELANEY SENDS HER REGARDS

It wasn't even the frustration borne of a wrongly accused man. Harmann could no longer reassure himself with that status.

Innocent.

It had been a week ago, as he crawled through the depths of that last glass of bourbon that, alone in the confines of the office, he'd asked himself that question, the one he'd been avoiding for three years.

Did I kill Mavis Delaney?

He no longer needed to close his eyes to see the scene. The Harmann of three years ago leaned through the shattered doorway, Glock in a two handed grip. He fired. The shooter died.

But he'd fired again, he knew he had even though he couldn't remember counting the rounds as they left the barrel. He'd seen the other two suspects and had fired a couple of shots towards them.

Towards Mavis Delaney.

Oh God, did I kill Mavis Delaney?

He reached for the drawer in his desk, opening it to reveal the black leather of a bible, a book he'd not turned to in decades. He pulled it out, laying the worn cover reverently on the wood before him, scattering a handful of the letters.

Oh God-

The door crashed open and Moore stood there, Finnick behind her. Her eyes quickly took in the scene, the letters across the desk, the bible.

"Harmann..."

"It's nothing." he swept the bible off the desk, back into the drawer and roughly kicked it shut "Weren't nothin'."

Moore's mouth hung slightly open in shock. She began to speak but Finnick who'd been behind her and hadn't seen the small drama barged past.

"Harm, brace yourself. The DA has signed Brooke's release. He's made parole."

"What?"

"He's getting out today-"

"He's got two more years!"

Finnick shook his head. Behind him, Kathy was hovering in the doorway "He's out. They're lettin' him go."

"No!" Harmann erupted onto his feet, slamming his fists on the desk "That bastard has to pay for this! He hijacked a goddamn airplane, stole millions of dollars and he gets out after three fuckin' years? That ain't justice!"

"Sir -" Kathy stuttered from behind Finnick.

"Harm, it's the system. You know what DA's are like. She-"

"I thought she was tryna improve our image? Not fuckin' empty jail cells! Stupid goddamn bitch!"

"Sir! Director Harmann!" Kathy's voice was insistent and to everyone's shock, she pushed past Finnick to lay a letter on Harmann's desk where it fell like a lead weight, identical to the others scattered across the wood "It's another one."

Harmann stared at the innocent looking slip of paper, his lip curling in disgust. Abruptly, he swept it off the desk onto the floor where it came to rest at Moore's feet. She sighed, bent down and scooped it up, tearing the paper open.

"Mavis Delaney send her fuckin' regards again?" Harmann snarled.

Moore had gone white, the color contrasting sharply with her red hair "No. It's..." she handed it mutely to Harmann.

THREE YEARS WAS NOTHING TO HOW LONG YOU'LL BURN FOR MAVIS DELANEY

"Brooke."

A savage light filled Harmann's eyes, the same predatory gleam that had signalled the end of freedom for hundreds of crooks over the years. He looked from Finnick who was just catching up to Moore who had already got it. She was wide eyed, shocked by the intimate emotion on Harmann's face. All these weeks of strain, of worry and frustration and now they knew. She gave him the smallest of nods.

"He gets out this afternoon?" Harmann flicked a glance at his watch "Let's go welcome him back to the world."

CHAPTER 42

"Alright, Brooke. You're still a prisoner until you pass the walls of this facility. Up 'til then, I want you to follow protocol, keep your damn mouth shut and pretend like you still got another two years. You got it?"

"Yes, Sir." Charlie could not keep the grin off his face and despite the Warden's harsh words, he saw the happiness reflected there. The warden was a decent man, he'd learned, focussed on rehabilitation. In the three years he'd been confined here, Charlie had seen hardened felons empowered with responsibility, education and purpose and he'd been quietly impressed at the efficiency of the system. There were no gangs, no violence and no corruption. The CO's were fair, if firm and often friendly with their charges. As he passed through hallways with applause and cheers from the other inmates ringing in his ears, he reflected on how spotlessly clean the place was. Floors mopped, walls white and air conditioners humming quietly in the corners.

"This way, Brooke."

They turned a corner, arriving at the processing hall, a long, low ceilinged building that everyone in the prison had seen with two doors, imaginatively marked 'IN' and 'OUT'. Charlie grinned as he followed the Warden through the 'OUT' door.

Two Correctional Officers waited inside, a plastic box sealed with forensic tape on a wide table before them. Charlie stopped in front and folded his hands neatly in front of him, as per prison regulations.

"Do you, Charlie Brooke consent for us to unseal your personal belongings that they may be returned to you in accordance with your rights as dictated under state law?" the CO read from a printed sheet.

"I do, Sir."

"Sign here."

Charlie scrawled his signature at the bottom of the page and the CO produced a box cutter, slicing through the tape. He leaned in, looking at the neat suit he'd worn for the trial. His wallet, cell phone and keys were placed atop although they'd moved around some when the box had been carried. A black Glock 19 sat in an IWB holster atop, the magazine removed.

"I'll return the firearm when you leave the premises." Warden explained "That's prison policy."

"Alright, Warden."

Charlie dressed in the suit, noting the fit remained the same. He smiled quietly to himself, grateful for the regimented exercise routine he'd kept up on the inside. Warden scooped up his Glock and held it to his chest before gesturing for Charlie to head to the opposite door, stepping through into the sunlight and freedom.

"Here you go, Mr Brooke." Warden handed him the Glock and Charlie took it with a smile, slapping the magazine into place and carefully stowing it in his waistband. Charlie held his hand out "Goodbye, Warden."

"Goodbye, Charlie. I hope we don't meet again, in the kindest of ways."

"Oh, I don't plan to." the two men smiled at each other as the Warden looked at something behind him.

Charlie turned to see the greatest sight God had ever put onto the earth. Yvonne ran from the parking lot, their two kids bouncing along behind her. She leapt at her husband and Charlie scooped her up, holding her legs around him as he kissed her warm skin, inhaling that wonderful feminine scent.

"I love you."

"I love you. I'm home now. All over."

Then the kids wanted daddy and he bent down, scooping them both up under an arm and roaring with laughter as they squealed and shouted.

They headed to the car, eager to put distance between the prison and their lives, to leave the memory behind. In the parking lot, a tall, sharply dressed man leaned against a plain looking sedan. His eyes were hidden behind sunglasses, but Charlie felt the jolt of recognition as they saw each other.

"Tagg."

"Charlie."

They shook hands warmly as Casey emerged from the sedan with his camera. He leaned back against the car for a stable purchase and nodded to Tagg.

"How does it feel to be free, Mr Brooke?"

"Damn good, Tagg. Damn good." Charlie grinned, the light glinting off his white teeth as he basked in the heat.

"What do you plan to do with your freedom?"

"Oh, I got an idea or two." Charlie nodded as the squeal of tyres and the revving of an engine sounded. Dust spilled up from the highway as a car, a sedan like Tagg's took the turn for the prison at high speed. They watched as it raced up the winding road before screeching to a halt in the parking lot.

Harmann erupted from the front door as Moore fumbled with her seatbelt. Finnick came after them at a sedate pace as Charlie turned to his wife.

"Wait in the car, honey. Get the AC runnin', huh?"

"I don't –" Yvonne began but her husband cut her off, steel in his tone behind the smile.

"Remember what we talked about, huh? Get the kids in the car, honey. I'll be right over." Charlie kept the smile broad on his face although his tone was cold as ice.

Harmann held the note in his hand, the white paper flapping in the sunlight as he waved it like a weapon at Charlie. The black text stamped across it bore the final anonymous message "You think this is fuckin' funny, huh? Think you can play me? You think you fuckin' won?"

Charlie grinned, appearing totally at ease "I know I did."

"I could bust your ass right now for harassment."

Charlie held up his hands in mock surrender "Oooh. Scary."

"You're a goddamn asshole, Brooke!" Harmann had stepped close to the big former Ranger, his teeth gritted "I'm comin' for you, you motherfucker! I'm gonna get you this time and you're goin' back inside for good!"

"Oh yeah? For what? I didn't do nuthin'!"

"The money you stole - I'm gonna find it! I'm gonna get it back and when I do, I'll find somethin' to pin on you!"

"You mean the money that Dunn stole?"

"You lying motherfucker!" Harmann's voice had fallen to a sibilant hiss as he stared up at Charlie, venom loaded into every syllable "I'm gonna find that cash - I know you know where it is! - and when I do, I'm gonna prove it was you that stole it, that masterminded this whole damn thing. Hell, maybe I'll even prove it was you that took a shot at me that day!"

Charlie's face turned cold "If I took a shot at you, you'd be dead."

Harmann stepped back a pace, happy he'd provoked the big man "Oh yeah? You think you're tough?"

"Tough enough that I don't need to murder old ladies to prove how big my dick is."

Red light flashed at the edge of Harmann's vision and before he could form a coherent thought, he'd punched Charlie in the chin. A swift hook which knocked the big man back a step. His hands came up to defend himself but then abruptly, he lowered them. Harmann snarled and followed up with his left, shooting a cracking hit across Charlie's nose, baring his teeth in terrible satisfaction as he felt the cartilage break and blood spray.

"Harmann!" Moore and Finnick leapt forwards even as Charlie fell backwards, Harmann now standing over him and raining blows down. They seized an arm almost simultaneously and tugged him backwards. Finnick tripped over Charlie's prone leg and staggered, losing his grip.

There was a click, audible even over the sound of laboured breathing and Finnick, with a litheness he'd not possessed in years flung himself back as Harmann slashed at him with his small black Wilson Folding knife.

"Harmann!" Finnick fell back onto his ass as Moore stepped sharply back.

Harmann raised his shoe and swung it once, twice, a third into Charlie's ribs. The black man curled over in agony, a thin, reedy sound emanating from his lips where blood poured from his shattered nose.

"Harmann!" Moore was yelling, frozen in a moment of indecision.

Then Harmann dropped to one knee, placed a flat hand on Charlie's face and swung the knife overarm into the big man's ribs.

"No!" wailed a female voice and Moore turned to see Yvonne Brooke, sprinting towards them from the car from where her two children stared in horror.

Moore reacted, finally. She drew her Glock and realised that with his back to her, Harmann would not react to the threat before he killed Brooke. She stepped close, seized the back of his collar and pistol whipped him as hard as she could, ringing his skull like a bell and feeling the shock of the vibration travel up her arm. It worked and Harmann pitched sideways to lie opposite Charlie in the dust.

Shouts sounded from the prison and an alarm began to ring. Correctional officers appeared in the doorway of the In/Out building and raced towards them, one of them carrying a shotgun which he pumped as he ran.

Moore stood over Harmann, pistol in a two handed grip as she covered him but he was groggy, not knocked out but dazed as Yvonne fell to her knees beside Charlie and pressed both hands over the wound on his side which was pumping blood.

"Medic!" yelled Finnick's voice as he too rushed to Charlie "Moore!" he snapped at her "Cuff that motherfucker!"

"On your front! Move!" snapped Moore and Harmann slowly responded but as he rolled, he caught sight of Tagg who was crouching behind his sedan.

Tagg, with his camera.

Who had filmed the whole thing.

"You motherfucker!" Harmann jerked back into alertness and kicked at Moore's knee which buckled. She'd holstered her gun while she drew the handcuffs and so she went down hard, unarmed and sprawled in the dust of the parking lot as Harmann staggered towards Tagg.

Who, impossibly, ignored him, instead staring at his phone screen, the only sign of tension his white knuckles gripping the case.

Casey, however, stood up behind his friend and in a well-practiced movement, drew the Glock 17 he'd purchased three years ago on Harmann's advice and pointed it straight at the Detective's face.

Harmann froze, anger, revulsion and fear fighting for space on his face.

"Done!" shouted Tagg to no-one in particular.

Moore tackled Harmann, flattening him to the ground as Casey covered him with the pistol. Moore got his hands cuffed behind his back and fought the urge to rabbit punch him in the back of the head as she read him his rights.

A revving engine and suddenly the prison ambulance was there. Charlie, the clothes cut away from his upper body was already being loaded onto a gurney, his eyes scrunched up with pain and his side covered in tight white dressings, glaring in the sun. Yvonne sobbed beside him, but Moore caught his eye as he was carried by the CO's into the back of the truck and to her surprise, he nodded, his gaze coming to rest on Harmann who was face down in the dirt, still and silent, only the rapid rise and fall of his chest signifying that he still lived.

"He's okay. He's okay." Finnick was standing beside her but his words didn't seem to be directed at her, or to anyone "I stopped the bleeding, think it missed the lung. He's gonna be okay." he was convincing himself that the assault was not going to turn into a homicide.

A car door opened and they turned to see Tagg stowing his camera equipment. The sight seemed to jolt Finnick out of his adrenaline fuelled panic and he stepped across to the young reporter.

"I need to seize this equipment." Finnick began, expecting the young man to argue but to his surprise, Tagg mutely handed the camera over. Moore raised her eyebrows at the acquiescence.

Sirens sounded as local law enforcement began to converge on the scene. A second ambulance arrived but Moore didn't think it would be needed. She looked down at Harmann who had gone totally still, his eyelids blinking occasionally.

She looked from him to Finnick, to Yvonne Brooke who was now pulling out of the lot and racing after the ambulance and simply stood and stared. The Warden was now approaching from the nearest prison building with a face like thunder and she heard Finnick groan.

"What a goddamn mess."

A sheriff's deputy arrived and Moore found herself grateful for the distraction, identifying herself and relaying the story, trying to ignore the look of disbelief on the officer's face. By nightfall, she realised, this would be all over the state, even without Tagg's footage.

Where was Tagg?

His car started just as the thought occurred to her and she watched in stupefied amazement as he and Casey vanished onto the highway.

"I never thought he'd do that." Finnick had left the Warden who was managing his own staff and come to stand by her, watching as Harmann was bundled into the back of a squad car.

She shook her head in mute agreement.

"He was always an asshole but that made him a good cop."

Silence, this time.

"You think Brooke provoked him? All this stuff about the Delaney woman? You think he sent those letters?"

Moore cleared her throat which was now dry with dust from the dozens of feet scuffing around "I think that if you try to spin the narrative that the black man provoked the cop into attempted murder, you'll give them the rope they need to hang you, Sir."

Finnick swallowed hard, dipping his head as he accepted the truth "Sorry. I wasn't thinking straight."

"Mmm."

Finnick took a deep breath "We'd better get things going by the book." he moved to stand in front of her "I want you to sit in the car right now and write your report. Got it?"

"Yessir."

"I'm going to call the DA. God help me." Finnick shook his head in sadness and pulled out his cell, turning away.

Moore reached the car and sat down, pulling out her notepad. Her hands shook as the adrenaline faded and she began to write, her penmanship shoddy.

Detective Harmann lost his damn mind she wrote before scrawling a line through that. She tried several more times but nothing professional came to mind. Instead, Moore lowered her face into her hands and shook her head back and forth. Charlie's face appeared in her mind's eye, standing there with his hands lowered, just taking the beating.

Goddamn. You smart son of a gun.

She imagined the big man lying in the ambulance, chuckling to himself even as he bled. She wondered just how much of this he'd predicted.

And why?

What did Charlie have against Harmann?

Frowning, Moore pulled out her phone and scrolled through the contacts before dialling one. It purred a few times before a chirpy voice answered "Well, hello there ma'am. What can I do you for, now?"

"Mitch? I need those records from your guy in the military. No - I don't care what it takes. Make the call. Right now."

CHAPTER 43

Tagg and Casey pulled up in the parking lot outside the makeshift studio. Casey sat with his hands on the wheel for a long moment as Tagg stared at the glove compartment in front of him. Neither man said anything.

Eventually, the beating sun made sitting still impossible and so Tagg made the first move, swinging open the door and climbing slowly out.

Casey followed, unlocking the studio and stepping into the cool interior. Without a word, he opened the small refrigerator and drew out two glass bottles of craft beer, snapping the tops off and handing one to Tagg. Both men drank deeply.

"Hell of a day, man." Casey shook his head.

"Glad you bought that gun." Tagg nodded.

"Me too. Whew. Good advice, huh?"

Tagg forced a snort at the irony "You ready?" he asked, nodding at the new workstation that lined one wall. An expensive Mac sat with the footage from the prison yard already downloading from the cloud, the software adding it to the existing project on the screen. Even from across the room the title could be read.

'DETECTIVE HARMANN'S REIGN OF TERROR'

"We got him." Casey muttered to himself.

"Oh yeah. We got him." Tagg stood up and led the way over to the screens where they both prepared to complete the final step in the laborious editing process. Tagg shot a glance at a small photo on the adjacent wall, over the spot where he'd once interviewed Harmann.

The photo showed a smiling woman with odd little glasses

balanced on her nose and elegantly coiffed curls. Beneath it were two dates, some seventy years apart above the legend 'RIP MAVIS DELANEY'.

CHAPTER 44

The state Attorney General led the way through the hospital corridors, her heels clicking on the shining floors as Finnick dragged his heels behind her, his head slumped over. He barely noticed the luxurious paintings on the walls, cleverly designed so they matched the medical equipment bolted on here and there. Nurses and doctors moved quietly through this wing, aware that more than half the hospital funding came from the patients in this wing alone.

That SATA had put Charlie Brooke up in here had not been questioned by anyone from the AG to the expenses team who simply approved the invoices, striking swathes of Finnick's budget. He could not argue and it was shame and guilt that made him hang back like a naughty schoolboy as the AG stopped outside the room with Brooke's name on the door and knocked smartly.

"Come in."

And there he was. The room was large, several plush armchairs gathered around a sci-fi version of a hospital bed with a smooth leather headboard and a water cooler bolted to the sides.

"Attorney General, I presume?" said Charlie Brooke, lying swathed in bandages on the bed. His eyes were bright, undimmed by pain medication and as Finnick followed the AG, he saw that a thin, tough looking woman dressed in a no-nonsense business suit stood on the far side of the bed.

"Mr Brooke, how are you?" the AG was all smiles and pleasantries, as was her job. The suited woman was Emmeline Vance, a lawyer from the VA with a Ranger lapel pin and a significant looking briefcase.

Finnick swallowed nervously.

"How are you finding the facilities here, Mr Brooke?"

"Oh, very pleasant, thank you. The TV is magnificent." Charlie pointed at the oversized black screen on the far wall.

"I'm glad that you're comfortable. I cannot even begin to explain how sorry I am for what has happened to you. I'm here to reassure you that I - that is Director Finnick and myself - are handling this case personally and will represent your cause."

"Well, that's mighty kind of you." Charlie shot them both a grin as Finnick nodded "However, thing is, I wanted to talk to you today because it seems I have a deal that may benefit us both."

The AG's ears pricked up like a stalking predator. Finnick knew that she would do whatever was needed to keep the crime covered up. Harmann would be dealt with, for sure, but the AG had spent her two years in office working to reshape the agency in her image and Harmann's assault on Charlie Brooke was a torpedo in her plans.

Charlie's lawyer, Emmeline, picked up a remote and flicked on the oversized TV. A video came into focus, two men wrestling in a dusty parking lot.

"Oh God..." Finnick recognised the footage of Harmann and Brooke, wincing and flinching as Harmann drove his knife into Brooke's side.

On the bed, Charlie Brooke remained impassive, turning only to see the reaction of the AG who rounded on Finnick.

"I thought this was seized?"

Vance stepped forward, her tone smooth and professional "Ma'am, this footage was sent to us from an anonymous source -"

"Tagg." put in Finnick.

"- who, after a conversation with Mr Brooke has agreed not to release the footage."

Even the AG knew that wasn't the full story.

Charlie spoke up "In return for something from you."

"That's blackmail." protested Finnick, before he could stop

himself.

"No, Director Finnick." Vance shook her head "It's a type of plea deal. It's perfectly legal."

"Ma'am?" he asked the AG but she ignored him.

"Go on, Mr Brooke."

"See -" Brooke shifted uncomfortably, wincing slightly in pain "- see, seems to me that we can help each other out. I'm willing to drop these charges - all of them - against Detective Harmann if you'll end the case that I know your fiscal team is working on."

Finnick frowned, a terrible realisation settling over him "You want us to stop looking for the money you stole?"

"I stole? That *Dunn* stole. Look - I think we can all agree that those companies that lost money have had their insurance pay outs? Dunn is gonna hang and-"

"And you get away with all that cash? Goddamn!" snarled Finnick but the AG put a hand up, silencing him.

"Mr Brooke -"

"Let me remind you." Charlie continued as though the AG hadn't spoken "Mohsin Singh was also let go by Director Finnick's agency because your man Harmann tortured him in an interrogation room."

"Allegedly." put in Vance.

"Allegedly. Right. But say if we had some footage of that? And then there's this business of Harmann and that old lady that was killed a few years back now. There's some footage of that too - publicly available now - and we had a couple'a experts from the VA take a look at Harmann's angle of shootin' there. Seems to me that he may well'a shot that old lady." Charlie affected a confused frown and looked at Finnick "Say, Director, wasn't that investigated by your agency? I seem to remember reading the public report some years back. A Detective Mitchell looked into it. I remember noting at the time how he was such a prestigious Detective and he'd served with the agency on a number of key cases. Some, in fact, that were led by Detective Harmann. Ain't that crazy how he didn't pick up that the bullet trajectories lined up?"

"This is blackmail!" Finnick's sympathy had evaporated "Look, what happened to you was wrong but we will prosecute Harmann by the book! Not by some shady plea deal that-"

"Shut up, Director." snapped the AG.

If she'd pulled out a pistol and shot him between the eyes, Finnick would not have been more surprised. He gaped at her, astonished and unable to form a sentence.

The AG ignored him, instead smiling sweetly at Charlie "Mr Brooke, you understand that the Fiscal team has been working on that case for nearly three years? It's not as simple as telling them to just 'stop'."

"Sure. Vance?" Charlie gestured at his lawyer who cleared her throat.

"As Mr Dunn has already been convicted of the thefts along with his other crimes, we've reviewed the court documentation and I think if we take a circumstantial interpretation, we can close the case based on the fact that Mr Dunn has been apprehended and is facing the maximum sentence." she handed a typed letter to the AG who took it, reading the wording carefully.

It was preposterous, of course it was and Finnick glowered at Brooke. It would take more than a liberal interpretation of court finding to pin the case on Dunn! The only person who would have the authority to approve such a step would be the Governor, or perhaps the AG herself.

"Okay." said the AG. She produced a fountain pen and signed the page with an elaborate flourish as Finnick stared in horror "Director? Would you make the call to the Fiscal team, please?"

Finnick felt one by one the pillars that supported reality come crashing down. In a dream like state, he took his cell phone out and made the call, speaking in a faint tone. He ignored the disbelief on the other end of the call, simply hanging up mid-protest. When he was done, he replaced the cell in his jacket pocket and stood, blinking stupidly.

"And so, you'll promise not to release those details, Mr Brooke?" the AG was all smiles as though she had not just broken the law.

"It's on the paper -" Charlie picked it up and read the wording to the AG "... solemnly promise not to release said video and indeed, to do everything in my power to prevent its release."

"Alright. Mr Brooke, I wish you a speedy recovery. Director?" the AG swept from the room and Finnick stumbled after her.

"Ma'am! Was that even legal?"

"Yes."

"But - but that man is going to get away with millions of stolen dollars!"

"So?" she was walking fast and Finnick had to hurry to keep up "Charlie Brooke's story could bring the entire agency, not to mention the state government crashing down. And besides, he wasn't the mastermind of the crimes, he was coerced into helping Dunn."

"Ma'am -"

"You saw the same trial I did, Finnick! Mr Brooke was a victim as much as anyone else!"

"What about the money, ma'am?"

She shrugged. Actually shrugged! As though tens of millions of dollars did not matter "The insurance paid out, didn't it? No-one got hurt. Need I remind you that Brooke was nearly killed by Harmann? This is about the moral choice, Finnick! We're in the wrong here!"

"But, ma'am!" exploded Finnick "You've let that man get away with stealing more than twenty million dollars? What if he isn't an innocent victim? What if he masterminded the whole thing?"

The AG stopped, turning to smile condescendingly at him as he stood lamely in the corridor "Oh, please. Finnick, this is a done deal. That man is no more a criminal mastermind than you are. Now, he may have dropped the charges against Harmann, but I want to see the results of your investigation on my desk by tomorrow. Got it?"

Finnick gaped at her, shaking his head in astonishment.

"Finnick! By tomorrow!"

She turned and left.

CHAPTER 45

Harmann paused at the street corner in a patch of sunlight. He wondered how long it would be before he could no longer do such a simple act when he chose, where he chose. The very principle of freedom, the same right his great grandfather had fought for in the civil war, had never seemed so poignant, so fragile.

His usually sharp appearance was fraying at the edges. A small tear in the knee of his pants, a broken shoelace, awkwardly knotted. His custom designed jacket was in a lock-up somewhere, impounded as evidence.

Finnick had his badge and his gun. The bastard had demanded them, holding his hand out like a pissed schoolteacher confiscating a pack of gum. Harmann hadn't said a word as Finnick had coldly told him about the investigation. Suspended with no pay. He wasn't sure that was even legal.

Harmann had been surprised when the deputy had let him out of the jail cell they'd tossed him into. For a brief moment, he'd assumed the agency had posted his bail but instead, the deputy told him the charges had been dropped and Finnick had explained the deal the AG had signed. In a way, that made it all worse. The thought of Charlie Brooke laughing over his stolen millions left a terrible coldness inside of Harmann. He wondered when someone would charge him with a crime – negligence or something similar. How long a prison sentence he'd get. He'd run through the first night in the penitentiary in his head over and over, guessing where the first attack would come from. An ex-cop, no matter what he'd done was fair game to the incarcerated population and Harmann doubted even the

CO's would give him protection.

But, it seemed, prison was not for him. Instead, he would be jobless. Middle aged, no pension, his house gone and no job. No wife. No family. Not even his gun to take his own life.

And it was all Charlie Brooke's fault.

What in the hell had he ever done to that man? Harmann knew that Brooke had set him up. Him and that bastard Tagg. He'd stared in disbelief at that interview they'd done in the prison, Brooke's gloating face spinning lies for the camera. The smug reporter, knowing his career was made.

And it was then, seeing the two of them together that Harmann had begun to appreciate the scale of the whole thing. Tagg, Brooke and Dunn. All rolled up together into a lead weight targeted straight at he, Harmann. But why? For what? There was no answer and Harmann surprised himself at his lack of rage. Instead, he just felt numb.

The crossing light went green and Harmann obediently began to walk. The midday sun beat down on his head and he tried not to think of the air-conditioned interior of the car Finnick had seized. An old black man passing the opposite direction peered at him intently and Harmann shifted his sunglasses a little lower on his nose, distorting the shape of his face.

"Ain't you that cop from the news?"

From the news? What had he done now? Harmann hurried on, ignoring the old man. Sweat soaked the back of his dress shirt and his pits stank. A bar loomed ahead, promising a TV and he ducked in, grateful to be out the sun even for a moment.

"Help you?" the barman called but Harmann ignored the man, turning his back to stare at the screen where his own face floated next to an image of Mother Mercy Hospital, just a block from here.

"... A match made in hell, two rivals on opposite sides of the law who seem to have switched sides!" the newscaster had relish in his voice, curling Harmann's lip in disgust "Seems that Detective Harmann of the SATA who famously put Brooke in jail for a spree of crimes took it upon himself to assault Mr Brooke as he was getting out of jail, sending him instead to the hospital. Rumours have flown but we should stress that as of right now, there is no concrete evidence of this although SATA have confirmed that Detective Harmann has been suspended pending an investigation ordered by the State Attorney General herself."

Harmann had heard enough. He left the bar, ignoring the protest from the barman and hurried on. That he was a block from the hospital was no coincidence, he'd found himself wandering ever closer that day as, with no job and nothing to do, he'd wandered the streets, needing to be active.

He rounded a corner and the white walls of the hospital came into sight. A group of reporters were already gathered at the entrance and he ducked to avoid being seen. His cell chose that moment to peal loudly, scaring the hell out of him. He'd forgotten he had the damn thing in his pocket.

"Harm?" the voice was Mitch and Harmann merely grunted in response "Harm, it's Mitch. I've got Moore here." a pause.

"Hello, Harmann." Moore sounded tired. More than that, she sounded pissed.

"What?"

"Where are you?"

"Out."

"Right. We called at your place."

"Well, I'm not there."

"Yeah." Mitch sounded uncomfortable "Anyway, Finnick said we weren't to speak to you, so I'd appreciate you keepin' this conversation under your belt."

Harmann said nothing but Mitch continued anyway.

"Anyway, this is a courtesy call for old times' sake. I know you'll be lookin' for an endin' and I thought I'd give it you. Long story short, my buddy up in the military called a buddy of his in the Rangers and they wouldn't give him Brooke's record but he was able to read a few key details out over the 'phone."

Harmann said nothing. Mitch would speak or he would not speak. It wouldn't change a thing.

"Yeah - turns out Brooke was adopted as a kid - changed his

name back to his birth name when he joined the military. Get this - the adoption paperwork was filled out by -"

"Mavis Delaney." Harmann sighed as he said it, the final chunk of the puzzle settling into place.

"Huh? You know that already?" Mitch was confused but Harmann was done with Mitch and he shook his head, something approaching a smile twitching the corners of his mouth.

"Moore? You there?"

"I'm here." her voice dripped with ice.

"You're a damn fine piece of ass, Moore. Hope someone gets in them panties one of these days." Harmann hung up, walked a couple of steps, then turned the cell off and tossed it into the neat row of box hedge that marked the boundary of the hospital grounds. He wouldn't need it anymore.

The half-smile still twitching at his lips, he shook his head in amazement as he rolled his sleeves up and began to walk slowly towards the reporters.

CHAPTER 46

"You got everything, honey?"

Yvonne's voice was calm and collected. This time it was just the two of them, the kids were already waiting for them where they were going.

"Sure." Charlie stood up, a new cell phone in his hand. He had nothing else with him.

"Alright." Yvonne led the way down the hallway, smiling her thanks to the nurses who wished Charlie well. The hospital was big and they wove their way through the maze of signposted wards and halls as Charlie limped along, one side still heavily bandaged.

His cell rang. Charlie glanced at the screen and smiled "Hello, Tagg."

Tagg spoke a few words and Charlie glanced at a column of signposts on the nearest wall. He gestured to Yvonne and they set off towards the exit Tagg had suggested, away from the baying crowd of journalists.

They emerged, five minutes later into the bright sunlight to see Tagg and Casey standing waiting by the box hedge. Tagg greeted Charlie with a smart handshake and nodded to Yvonne.

"I s'pose it's all done now?"

"All done." Charlie smiled. A second later, they all wheeled around as a shout of recognition sounded and the herd of reporters came sprinting around the corner, lugging cameras and microphones as they sweated under the relentless sun.

"Here..." Charlie pulled Tagg a step closer, so his back was to the box hedge. Charlie stood as close to him as possible as Yvonne sheltered behind her husband's back.

"Mr Brooke! Charlie! Mr Brooke! Can you tell us what happened? Did Detective Harmann assault you? How do you feel about his suspension? Where are you going now? What happened to you?"

Charlie smiled and held up a hand for silence, the cameras of a dozen networks capturing every moment.

He turned to Tagg who held up a microphone "Mr Brooke, it's all very confusing to those of us here. There are a lot of rumours flying around. It seems that you and Detective Harmann have traded places on the side of good and bad. Can you tell us what happened?"

Ten feet away, hidden by the crowd of passers-by who had stopped to gawk at the sudden burst of action, Harmann stared incredulously. Surely Brooke was not about to throw it all away for a single interview?

"No fuckin' way!" he heard someone say and realised a moment later that it was his own voice. The woman in front of him turned around and shot him a poisonous look but Harmann ignored her, looking past to where Brooke smiled.

"I'm afraid the details of how I got my injuries are personal. I made a solemn vow not to reveal the cause to anyone."

"I understand that there is some video evidence of the event, something that would give us proof of the rumours we've been hearing?"

"I don't know nothin' 'bout that, Sir." Charlie smiled, looking benevolently around at the sea of cameras.

"Bastard." muttered Harmann, shaking his head as that strange smile played around his lips. He found himself moving forward as though in a trance, eyes fixed on Charlie Brooke.

"But if there was video evidence?" Tagg had a meaningful note in his voice, a pleading tone that raised more than one eyebrow in the pack of journalists.

Charlie turned to Tagg, looking the younger man in the eye and holding that strong gaze. After some time, he gave a single nod, his face sombre "I'd say, Tagg, that an enterprising young reporter might well be able to dig the truth out if he were so inclined."

Tagg swallowed hard, blinking behind his sunglasses "Thank you, Mr Brooke."

The press, Charlie forgotten, rounded on Tagg like a pack of hungry wolves. Tagg stepped forward as Charlie and Yvonne, hands clasped tightly together stepped between him and the box hedge, slipping towards the parking lot.

"Mr Brooke?"

Charlie turned at the voice but there was no surprise in his movement. Indeed, it seemed as though he'd been expecting it and he guided Yvonne back a step, putting space between them and Harmann as he stood before them.

Charlie's eyes travelled over Harmann's face, noting the stubble, the dishevelled hair and the unwashed shirt. He did not miss the twitch in Harmann's bloodshot eyes.

Harmann lunged forward.

Charlie stayed still.

A blur of movement from the side which Harmann caught in his peripheral vision. Thirty years of dangerous living took its toll and he flinched away, ducking as Yvonne stepped forward, a small handgun clutched in a professional grip.

"Back!" she snapped and Harmann stared at her in stupefied amazement.

Charlie grinned his white-toothed smile as Harmann looked up at him as Yvonne hovered, weapon drawn. No-one had noticed, their attention totally on the crowd of reporters now mobbing Tagg.

"You shot my Mom."

"I might have."

"I know you did."

Harmann shook his head "You couldn't have. No-one could tell for sure."

"It was your fault. You went into that robbery with those cameras, showin' off and acting like an ass. You got my Mom killed."

"It ain't -"

"It's your fault. You know it is." Charlie's eyes seemed to burn with a dark fire as Harmann watched "You know what she was doin' that day? The day you decided to prance around like some fuckin' moron in front of them TV cameras? She was emptyin' her savings. Gonna come live with us and put the money in a fund so her grandkids could go to college. And you killed her, you motherfucker."

Harmann just stood there, sweating in the sun.

Yvonne stepped closer to Charlie, gun still held in rock solid hands. Charlie nodded to her.

"Anyway, you killed my Mom, I ruined your life. You miserable asshole."

Harmann shrugged "I did what I did. Do you really feel like the good guy here? I ain't got nothin' left."

Charlie smiled and in that moment, Harmann saw something in the former Ranger's eyes, a darkness that had nothing to do with the color of the iris "See, that's your mistake, Harmann. You always thought you were the good guy. That meant I had to be the bad guy. Now the tables are turned, you think I must want to be the good guy. But I never claimed to be the good guy."

"But-"

"I'm the guy with twenty million dollars." the grin was back in place but there was no humour in it. Only hatred. "And you're gonna go to jail where they love cops *so* much." Charlie raised a hand, fingers shaped like a gun. He cocked the imaginary weapon and fired it making a 'pew' sound as he did so. Then he laughed, a great derisive guffaw and hooked his uninjured arm around his wife, leading her towards the waiting car and speaking loudly enough for Harmann to hear "C'mon, honey. Let's go watch that video you showed him."

"Oh, can we do the unedited version this time? The one where you can see my face?" Yvonne purred and the two of them howled with laughter as they climbed into their car, started the engine and pulled away.

Harmann watched them go, hands hanging by his sides as his mind slowly emptied of all feeling. He stayed there, standing and staring at the empty street long after they'd vacated it and long after the crowd of reporters had left to write up their reports.

He simply did not understand how he had lost.

EPILOGUE

Tagg

In the old days, Tagg reflected as Casey glanced nervously back at him from the swivel chair before the Mac, they'd have done this on a talk show, a studio audience gasping and oohing at every turn, but Tagg didn't know any talk show hosts he wanted to share this with.

Instead, he'd share the four videos on social media where the hashtags would send them spinning off into the roaring currents of cyberspace.

"Okay. All four ready to go."

"Have you tagged Smith in?"

"Yup. You wanna call him and say we're ready?"

"Sure." Tagg dialled the number of the former Ranger and the grizzled voice answered on the second ring "Mr Smith? We're ready to upload our footage. I just wanted to check you and your team are still willing to testify if it comes to that?"

"Sure. That sumbitch shot the lady, sure as anything."

Tagg let out a deep sigh "Thank you for all your help, Mr Smith."

"My pleasure."

The line went dead and Tagg nodded to Casey as the first video, this a lightly re-edited version of the raid he and Casey had followed along with three years ago. This time, the footage slowed as Harmann leaned around the doorframe and emptied his gun without aiming before cutting to the footage of Smith and his team, their bonafides floating beneath their faces, reporting their analysis that it had been Harmann's round that struck Mrs Delaney in the head.

The second, was a brief clip filmed from a concealed camera of Harmann kicking Tagg in the face, in this very studio. The clip was cut before Moore's face was revealed.

The third, came with an understanding from a certain red-haired Detective that this was the extent of their relationship and was lifted from an unmarked disk that in no way revealed that it was an illegal copy of interrogation room footage from the SATA control room, showing none other than Detective Harmann beating Mohsin Singh to a pulp.

The final, showed Harmann stabbing Charlie Brooke in the parking lot of the prison, making sure that Director Finnick was caught on the camera and Detective Moore, was not. A watermark disclaimer hung over the video, cleverly spaced so that it disrupted none of the footage, informing the reader that the footage was released without the consent of the victim but that he, Tagg, thought it in the public interest to share it, regardless of the implications.

The first video was shared a few thousand times in the first hour it was online. After all, the public had seen the Delaney raid before and it took some time before word spread that this was a new version and it held a terrible secret.

The second video was picked up by a human rights lawyer in LA who posted it to her Twitter feed four minutes after Tagg had released it. Within twenty minutes the few seconds of footage and the contextual text had reached a million views.

The third and fourth videos were uploaded within seconds of each other, dropping in to the already seething pool of righteous indignation that filled the different social platforms. Politicians were sharing them within ten minutes, journalists sent them worldwide and activists embedded them on websites in countries where social media was prohibited. Within ten minutes, these two alone had been shared over a million times. By the time ninety minutes had elapsed since Tagg had uploaded the first video, he'd stopped clicking the refresh button because the string of digits had lost meaning.

Instead, he and Casey sat and stared in fascination at the monster they had unleashed. They did not cheer, did not celebrate. Instead, the blood-soaked curls of an old lady filled Tagg's mind. He wondered where Charlie was now, his mind filled with visions of white sandy beaches and laughing children.

Harmann's face was on every new site, social feed and trending video. SATA and the AG were being mobbed for answers that Tagg knew they didn't have.

"Bastard." muttered Casey as Harmann's mugshot appeared on the news channel.

"Him, or Charlie?"

Casey could not answer that. After a minute, he went and fetched the last two beers from the cooler and handed one silently to Tagg who drank greedily.

"Did we do the right thing here?"

Casey shrugged. Drank some beer. Shrugged again "Dunn's gonna hang. Harmann ain't seein' the light of day anytime soon."

"Sure."

"Mavis got justice."

"Yup." Tagg nodded firmly. Of that point, he was certain.

Casey finished the beer, glanced once at the cooler then sighed and reached under the desk, producing a half empty bottle of tequila and two dented tin mugs.

"Here."

They sat together in silence as they drank, watching the news tear the world apart.

THE END

Printed in Great Britain
by Amazon

33752293R00108